# Thirty Three Good Mornings
# and other stories

D E Young

Published 2013 by arima publishing
www.arimapublishing.com

ISBN 978 1 84549 601 2
© D E Young 2013

Printed and bound in the United Kingdom
Typeset in Garamond 12

In this work of fiction, the characters, places and events are
either the product of the author's imagination or they are used
entirely fictitiously. Any resemblance to actual persons, living or
dead, is purely coincidental.

arima publishing
ASK House, Northgate Avenue
Bury St Edmunds, Suffolk IP32 6BB
t: (+44) 01284 700321
www.arimapublishing.com

for

Mrs. Malini Prasad, Consultant Gynaecologist West Suffolk Hospital
and Mr. Martin McNally, Consultant in Bone Infection and Limb
Reconstruction,

Nuffield Orthopaedic Hospital, Oxford.

who each gave me the chance to write

and Mrs. Katharine Thomas, who gave me the chance to publish.

# Contents

# Preface

In this first Collection of my Short Stories, I invite you, the reader, to find a place from which to see things differently. The uniqueness of place, its special atmosphere is, I believe, even more memorable than a narrative. These stories are situations distilled and presented in a minutely observed but open manner. Mine are stories of reminiscence, tragedy and paradox written over the course of two years whilst I recovered from two serious operations. Before my illness, I had not written at all, and my family was very surprised to find that I had discovered an occupation which gave me a smile on my face and a passion for a new-found craft.

I must thank my 'gentle readers', Margaret, Elizabeth, Francis, Joan, Sophie, my husband Alan, and my daughter, Naomi, for kind and robust comments when each story was ready. My thanks also to the Cathedral Community at Bury St. Edmunds, particularly Margaret Ellis, whose home visits made so much difference, to its Library volunteers, especially Ricky and Paul, and for the impetus of the Edmund Centre for Arts and Theology (ECAT) which launched its monthly lectures just when I needed to find the academic and creative spur to what I so enjoyed doing. Dr. Elizabeth Cook, the Writer-in-Residence, has been an inspiration.

D. E. Young, September 2013

# Mr. Howard's Doughnut

She had been assigned by the Civil Service to an area called London countryside, but Sandra did not know that at the beginning. It was an exciting job for her, leaving school as she had with good examination results and needing to live away from home for the first time. She set off for her first week's work, arriving on a quiet Sunday afternoon.

The small town clustered around its ancient crossroads and, like bristles off that Roman routemaster's brush, small side roads branched from its taut straightness, each reaching into Sandra's new awareness of countryside. As she looked ahead, walking steadily past turning after turning, the small amount of heat haze shimmered between what few elms dotted the receding hedgerows.

'Romans, or whatever nationality, marching into the unknown West', she thought, as she spotted her destination.

'At least I'm not doing that,' she half-smiled, keen to see her digs.

As she approached, the chunky set of villas off the High Road tidily appealed and number 37's clipped privet, confidently bulging towards the bay across the narrow front garden, spoke of a certain warmth and encouragement. She'd be happy here.

Mrs. Howard answered her knock. Her frock and cardigan were of an average, but the friendly, well-fed face above was filled with a wide smile of welcome.

'Come in, love. You must be Sandra,' she said.

'Yes, I'm Sandra Yates, Mrs. Howard. How do you do?' she said with a returning smile.

Inside, a darkened hallway which as a flat-dwelling Londoner Sandra had never seen before, stretched ahead.

Mrs. Howard led her down the narrow passage to the back of the cramped house, where a small kitchen was set up with a table to one side. This room led on to a scullery where a stolid wooden door opened onto a square of garden hardly much bigger than the privet-hedged front.

Sandra had never felt so stopped and bolted to a place. Her Council flat home was not roomy, but it was a few storeys up, light and airy, overlooking the tenants' allotments and a wide horizon. This house was a coop. No-one looked up at the sky.

'Hadn't they heard that sunlight is good for you?' she thought.

Things looked different upstairs where Sandra was shown her room.

It overlooked quite a few gardens at the back which each held an array of washing lines. Although the room was small with the single, high bed dominating, a small matching wardrobe and dressing table just fitted femininely enough to satisfy. Evidently, this and the kitchen would be home. No need to cook or clean. Mrs. Howard was paid to do it all, like an unknown mother in the dark background of her ideas of homemaking life. She'd be cleaning and cooking while Sandra was out, or keeping quiet if Sandra had to sleep during the day.

'I had the last newcomer from your place here,' Mrs. Howard said proudly, 'but you're the first girl I've known they've employed. You must be clever.'

Sandra admitted that she thought the exams were hard.

'Come six o'clock, Bert will be home. We'll all have supper then,' said Mrs. Howard, and she left Sandra to her thoughts.

Later that day Sandra found Mr. Howard a squat, comfortable looking man with a patient gaze and an eye on his wife as he spoke. He sat down on one of the kitchen chairs after the formal introduction.

'Up from London, then?' he said and touched his knife and fork on the table, responding to routine and his need for supper.

'Sit down here, Sandra. Bert'll eat supper with you about this time every day and if you or Bert are late you'll find your meal keeping warm in the oven.'

Sandra sat down and looked at Mr. Howard.

'Where do you go to work?' she asked as the plates came out of the oven and on to the table.

'I'm at the Vauxhall, Luton, like most round here,' he replied as he started to eat without waiting for her.

Sandra enjoyed his company for that half hour. Mr. Howard didn't need to say much to be sociable because Sandra found a way of overcoming her strangeness and feelings of home-sickness by talking to him almost non-stop about her family of two sisters.

Mr. Howard 'ummed and 'aahed' in the right places and then Sandra turned to find Mrs. Howard not there at all. Seeing her quizzical look, Mr. Howard remarked.

'She always goes off. Got her routine she has and it don't include us.'

His enigmatic reply to a question she hadn't asked gave her a sense of companionship oddly forged in this cramped kitchen with a working man's elbows on the thin table top.

'She has to get on with things, I suppose,' Sandra said by way of reply, and told him how her mother fed the family when they'd just got in from school.

'But two of us three are working now,' she concluded.

'That's nice,' said Mr. Howard, getting up to put his plates by the side of the sink. He took her plates too, and in the same way he eyed his wife, he looked at the door.

Sandra said goodnight and went upstairs to her room.

As it happened, Sandra had never thought of her parents as old, but Mr. and Mrs. Howard seemed so old. Sandra's natural reticence turned to something more like quiet astonishment as she gradually witnessed and grasped the routine of housekeeping in this seemingly timeless home.

Sandra's job was mathematical and logical. The thrill and skill of upper air physics and its down-to-earth meticulous compilation suited both her youth and aptitude. High up on the downs, the visual world of her chosen profession passed in a race of shifting patterns of cloud, wind and rain, the bread and butter of a meteorologist. Sandra never tired of looking up. There was no featureless progression in this job. She observed her mathematical world go by in real time. At the Howards', time was so straightforward it was as if the narrow house itself ordained it.

It was one early evening that Sandra returned from a day at work to find no-one in the house but herself. A note on the hall table read 'Gone to see a friend down the road. Bert's dinner in the pantry.'

Sandra assumed that Mr. Howard would be late in and went upstairs to wash and change. She came down to the kitchen with its smell of boiled potatoes, sat down at the small table and took the cover off her plate of food. It was a cold pork pie with salad and tomatoes, diced cold potatoes and sliced beetroot. A jar of chutney stood on the table and, as she took it, Sandra saw the two doughnuts on a single plate tucked round behind the jar.

All through her meal, as she slowly ate in the silent kitchen, Sandra thought about the doughnuts. After the spicy beetroot and chutney, a jammy sweetness would be very nice, not to say deserved, after a hard day's close work.

'But is one of them for Mr. Howard?' she thought and had no means of telling, short of getting up to examine the pantry with its many tins. His dessert could easily be something else he'd been told about when he left that morning. Her worrying continued.

'The two of them are on one plate, meaning that they are twin doughnuts for me.'

Single plates and double doughnuts took over her thoughts as she finished the final piece of pie leaving only a stalk end of a tomato on her plate.

'They do look quite small,' she said confidingly to herself, perplexed at such a dilemma. Dessert was usually an uncompromising apple pie and custard portion, easy to spoon and generously filling. She began the comparison as she picked up one of the doughnuts and bit into it. It was fresh and definitely bought today. It had a very tasty jam. Not feeling as filled as with apple pie, Sandra picked up the second doughnut and enjoyably ate it to finish her meal.

Next morning, Mrs. Howard was in the kitchen at breakfast instead of upstairs making the beds as usual. Mr. Howard was evidently having a lie-in for a late shift.

'Bert said he didn't have his doughnut last night,' said Mrs. Howard, looking sternly at Sandra as she entered. 'It was you as ate it, I suppose?'

'Yes,' said Sandra, 'I thought they were both for me as they were on the one plate.'

'Oh, did you now,' half glared the normally pleasant Mrs. Howard. 'Well, they weren't and Bert went short didn't he?'

'I'm sorry, Mrs. Howard.' Sandra's remorseful tone was genuine.

'I've got you both to feed and you've got to understand what's what. They only had them two in the shop and I knew I'd be rushing off to Nora's.'

Mrs. Howard looked flustered more than angry now. Things hadn't gone right at all and Sandra was to blame.

'Don't let it happen again,' she muttered as she turned to the kitchen sink to wash up.

Walking to work that morning Sandra's mind began to encounter all the consequences of doughnut taking. She'd have the rent raised or fall out permanently with the landlady. Mealtime portions might be minutely reduced over the weeks to pay for the offending object. Mr. Howard's meals would be enlarged in consequence of hers diminishing and he would become bloated and ready for a heart attack.

It was the next evening when they found themselves together that Sandra apologised.

'Don't worry about it, Sandra. I don't like doughnuts anyway. I was late off shift and it would have been as solid as a rock by the time I got to it. I'm glad you got it fresh.'

Sandra coughed lightly by way of agreement. Mr. Howard spoke again.

'You don't know her yet. How particular she is. You just wait. One day soon, you'll see what I mean.'

It was almost formidable how the doughnut had brought them together. Up to that moment, a matter of two or three months, Mr.

13

Howard was still at the reticent 'getting to know you' stage, which had been extended because of Sandra's unsocial hours and Mr. Howard's shifts at the motorcar factory. If she had bumped into him, it was nearly always something like;

'Stew again today! Can't she get some lamb chops for a change?'

Then, 'How was your day, Miss?' and Sandra would reply.

'Very busy, thanks, but I got out at lunch time.'

'More than I did', he'd reply tersely, but not now. On account of the doughnut, his commentary style of conversation eased up dramatically.

'We've been married for thirty two years and the two boys have grown up and gone. She's been a good'un, but you'll see what I mean quite soon.'

And quite soon it was.

Sandra was on her way down the High Street at six o'clock in the morning, returning from a busy night duty. The Senior Forecaster had been tiredly argumentative and so she was more than ready for breakfast and a good sleep.

It was a truly bright Friday morning in July. The High Road had only a dribble of traffic. Sandra couldn't help thinking of holidays but, now she was working, her soonest leave was in September.

As she opened the door to the house it knocked against an object behind it. Sandra looked to find it was a packed suitcase. Then Sandra saw that the front room door was open.

Closing the front door carefully in case of a rare visitor, Sandra peered into this formerly forbidden territory. In the bright light of the East-facing room, she blinked at Mrs. Howard who was firmly sat back in a comfortable armchair in the bay window. She was wearing a lightweight coat and holding a large handbag on her lap.

'Good morning, Mrs. Howard,' said Sandra in surprise. 'Are you off on holiday this morning?'

'No, Sandra. Bert's got today to work, but the coach leaves at eight o'clock tomorrow morning. I'm always ready early, just in case. Your meals are plated up for you and we'll be back from Bournemouth on Sunday at six in the evening.'

Mrs. Howard settled herself more firmly by way of dismissal and Sandra left the room to find her breakfast.

That evening, Mr. Howard nodded knowingly at her over an early supper.

'She always does this. Can you imagine what it was like when the boys were here? She's had sandwiches from her bag for today's lunch and supper and she'll dose off in that chair. It's her chair where she has to be ready in case.'

'In case of what?' Sandra just had to say.

'Well, you tell me. Perhaps the coach'll come early; the stop's just up the road, and she'll be first on or there'll be a hold up and she won't have to panic.'

'But she's ready more than a day before,' said Sandra, knowing that she could speak familiarly to Mr. Howard now.

'I know, but nothing's ever been able to change her. She's got to be ready in perfect order for the trip. Come Sunday lunch in Bournemouth, she'll be ready and waiting again. I'll be in the local bar.' He smiled awkwardly, letting Sandra into his whereabouts as opposed to his wife's.

Sandra wanted to mediate.

'At least you know where you stand.'

'Sit, more like,' smiled Mr. Howard. He was off on holiday after all.

A few weeks later, Sandra was told that there was a Saturday day trip coming up. Mrs. Howard was going with the Women's Circle. Mr. Howard and Sandra were in their usual routine.

It was just after supper on the Friday that Sandra rushed to Mrs. Howard in the front room.

'Come through,' she said urgently, 'your husband's fallen to the floor in the kitchen.'

Mrs. Howard rose quickly, put her bag down and went through in alarm.

Bert was on the floor, laughing silently that he'd got her 'out of that blessed chair!' He exploded with mirth that their plan had worked. Sandra stood back to watch.

'You demon!' Mrs. Howard really laughed, and she gently put her foot with its carefully polished shoe on the side of his head to pin him down. She stood like Britannia.

'I can wait like this,' she smiled. 'You can fetch my handbag, if you don't mind, Sandra.'

'That's my girl, Ethel,' said Mr. Howard as his wife helped him up, and all three laughed on the way back to the front room.

# Secrets

'Which one, Mum?' said Pete with a childish grin to his mother. 'Annie in Leicester or Steph in London?' He waved a different pack of letters in each hand.

'You kept on writing to them both?' said his mother. 'You're that artful, then, and now you're out of the Forces you've got a choice. What if they're disappointed in you?'

'No fear, Mum. I'll go for the Londoner first. She'll be streetwise.'

Pete made no secret of the fact that he had kept the flimsy letters written to him in Aden on his three year posting so as to go for a girl as soon as he got back. After all, why else would they write using the Forces befriending scheme?

'I hope you don't regret it,' said his mother. 'What's wrong with Leicester?'

'Nothing, Mum, but London's a bit more lively.' he replied.

'Yes, but Leicester's closer, You've got to save your money until a job comes up,' said Mrs. Elsie Brown as she turned to the sink.

'Oh, that's fixed up already, Mum, but the job's a bit of a secret. I'll be working near Stony Stratford for a month or two, then it's a move to the West country they say.' He reluctantly picked up a tea towel to help.

'Well, if it's electronics, you'll get on. You always were a clever one.' Mrs. Bates handed her newly returned eldest son a saucepan, saying, 'I don't know about all this, though.'

'It's my life, Mum,' he said as he flung down the tea towel, and then, demob happy, he took himself to London.

Steph's full figure and strawberry blonde hair brightened up her terraced London home and the elderly parents were proud of an only daughter who'd got herself a good secretarial job.

'I can't believe we've finally met up,' said Steph, touching her light-catching hair. Her hazel eyes were its exact match.

'I didn't know what to expect, but I'm glad I'm here. Shall we go to the cinema tonight?' said Pete.

'You bet,' was the reply and, 'Wait till I tell the girls.'

It wasn't a whirlwind, but as Annie in Leicester didn't get the half-promised visit, Steph took centre stage. She acted her part very well and their marriage came six months after his return to civvy street, despite all the advice about hasty promises and unwise investment given by the Commander as the lads left his section.

'Take it steady, if you do nothing else. Go slow. Digest.'

Impulsive Pete, no worse than that, it's true, paired up with Steph for better or for worse. She seemed really happy to have left London life behind her.

'It's great that you like Mum so much,' he said to Steph on one of their visits to his childhood home. 'She says you're a smiler.'

'Your Mum's about young enough to have a life of her own, especially with your dad gone.' said Steph in reply. 'My folks don't ever go out now. They've got nothing to talk about.'

With Pete's job in Cheltenham a decent wage, Steph had given up office work and stayed at home. It nagged at Pete for the first year.

'What do you do at home all day? Don't you want company?'

'I can't ask you what you're doing at work all day, can I?' she'd promptly reply. 'I'll do as I please.'

Pete felt he ought not to complain when Steph was expecting their first child in the following year of marriage.

Peter junior was born in the September and after a few weeks, Steph wanted to go over to Pete's mum.

'I'll stay till Christmas if I can,' she said with a smile.

'My younger brother has just left school, so it should be all right.' Pete said, but it would be quite a few months away from his young son. 'I'll get over at weekends. I should manage.'

Steph let an all too willing grandmother do the work. Mrs. Brown set out to show her the best ways with a son. She'd had three of her own. Nappies were washed separately, milk boiled up in a double saucepan only for that purpose. Pete had parted with a good bit of money for baby things, but Elsie Brown soon saw it all going on cigarettes and magazines.

'He needs you to pick him up when he cries,' said Elsie pensively one day, when it was quite clear that Steph was deaf to her own first child.

'It'll wait,' she said defensively. 'He can't have all his own way.'

It wasn't easy drying the nappies that wet winter. Elsie came to Peter's cot regularly.

'He's all wet, Steph. I thought I'd got yesterday's lot dried for you.' said Elsie, picking Peter up.

'I'll sort it in a bit,' said Steph with a yawn.

Elsie's generation had well-behaved babies in hand-knitted garments sitting up in hooded prams for neighbours to admire. Elsie didn't want to meddle in more modern ways, but Steph's attitude had to be brought to Pete's notice somehow.

It wasn't an easy Christmas at all. The young family was returning to their rented home in the New Year. Steph had overstayed her welcome, but if she couldn't be left with the child on her own, neglect would be a norm. Elsie spoke to Pete when he'd driven over to collect everything from the extended stay.

'She's not got a clue and she won't listen,' said Elsie fiercely. 'It doesn't matter what I say, she goes her own lazy way.'

'You always did too much for us,' laughed Pete. 'Steph'll get it together. She'll get in a group of mums back home. Peter's bigger now.'

He could be heard crying upstairs. He was almost five months and had been sitting up well, but Pete went up to find him banging his head on the side of the cot.

Back home in Gloucestershire, Pete was determined that Steph would settle to motherhood. When he came home in the evenings, Peter looked clean and was agile for his age.

'Had a good day with him, Steph?' he'd say. 'Did you get out at all? How's that friend of yours, Jenny?'

'She's gone off the boil, and no mistake. I get on by myself. I pushed Peter out to the shops,' was Steph's reply.

Pete went out with his friends from work on Friday nights. Steph didn't want to come, even though there was a neighbour quite happy to babysit. With Peter up and about more, walking well and talking enough, Pete thought Steph had her work cut out.

'Okay then, Steph. You watch TV, but keep an eye on Peter won't you? I noticed his forehead's got a bit of a bruise on it,' said Pete.

'He will stand up in the cot to wait for me, and he falls over as he jumps about. That's how he hit his head,' Steph said, and she met Pete's glare.

'Well, get up there a bit sooner, will you? You've got number two on the way and I don't want Social Services round here!' Pete's anger was real. He'd thought that another baby due at exactly two years after Peter would help Steph focus, but she couldn't keep the secret of her neglect of the eldest child from him any longer.

'I know you're getting tired now, but for heaven's sake, sort Peter out. We've agreed you'll go to mum's for the birth. She'll love that with Peter walking and all,' he said cheerfully.

'I'd really like to stay for Christmas, if she can stretch it,' said Steph. 'It'd be just like I did before.'

'Oh, all right, I'll ring her and see what she says, but I know I'm not off this Christmas. They're short-staffed.' Peter ran his hands through his thinning hair as he spoke.

'You've said that before,' scoffed Steph. 'If it's all so secret, it's a pity they can't keep more staff at just the time when secrets'll come out, when they drink too much down the pub.'

'That's none of your business,' said Pete and went to the 'phone.

It was at the pub a few weeks before that he'd met a woman named Carolyn. She caught his attention with her absent-minded gaze and body language just like his, pre-occupied.

'Penny for your thoughts?' She'd agreed to a sherry with him. He had asked in a gentlemanly fashion.

'It's not so much thoughts,' she said. 'I'm here to contemplate.'

'Don't you want a quieter place for that?' Pete smiled.

'It's too quiet at home, if that's what you mean,' smiled Carolyn in return as she sipped the sherry, and her face puckered a little.

'I've got a boy nearly two and another one on the way,' said Pete, 'I don't suppose I'll know the meaning of quiet for a while.'

It was the sense of quiet that drew the two together. Before long it was a quiet meal, a quiet day out, a quiet weekend and then, it was Christmas to themselves. Carolyn had no ties except her Bank Clerk husband. Pete had a squawling daughter, Helen, born in September.

Helen was one of those babies you knew had come into the world to create a storm. Up in Elsie's bedroom, which was the warmest, Helen made her lusty, loud appearance to a very satisfied midwife.

'You'll know you've got her,' she said with relish.

Peter was grateful for a girl, to help his wife mend her ingrained lazy ways. Surely a bright, pretty girl will change things, he had said to his mother rather sourly at the end of one weekend before he drove back in the late Autumn.

'You would think so, but you don't know so, Pete. I'll be keeping an eye before the New Year, but it's up to you after that.' she said, just wishing the baby could be a joy and not an outright worry. 'I can't for the life of me see how she does so little. Two kids and she can hardly get up from the television to see to either of them. You did choose the wrong one, Pete, and no mistake.'

'Don't go on about it, Mum. They're my kids, too,' replied Pete and turned to go as he usually did.

And he went, of course, to Carolyn for a Christmas break which both she and he lied about. She was told nothing of his job, so with secrecy as an everyday commitment, a few nights and every other weekend served him well. Carolyn had a conveniently ill grandmother at a safe distance and with an even safer amount in the elderly lady's Bank balance to make the caring visits an obligation. Jeff, the husband, saw that, too. It was not as if he had all the weekend to drive her over. Banks work on Saturdays. They make no secret of that.

It was between Christmas and New Year, those days all but emptied of turkey but likely to be filled with booze, that Pete and Carolyn met at Pete's for an evening meal. Carolyn would need to be back home that night as usual, so it couldn't be lengthy, but she lighted candles for the takeaway and dished up on a large lazy-susan for a clever effect.

'I like it this way,' she said to Pete. 'It shows the meal off better.'

'I like the wine to open me up,' said Pete. 'It's been a long week and I'm going over to Mum's tomorrow for the New Year pick up.'

'How's the new baby now?' said Carolyn, toying with a couple of serving spoons.

'Oh, as well as can be expected. Mum's 'phoned and says Peter is pleased with her.' said Pete and began to serve Carolyn. 'Some of this?'

'Yes please,' she paused. 'Would you like another one? I've got one for you. Give me a bit more. I'm eating for two.' Her excited eyes looked at Pete's just as he dropped the serving spoon.

'I don't believe it! Carolyn, what are you going to do?' He realised he'd put far too much on her plate and the spoon had spattered sauce on to the table.

'What do you mean, 'do'? I'm not doing anything,' Carolyn said casually and took the spoon to tidy up her plate.

'This wasn't meant to happen, though, Carolyn. No, I won't have any of that,' insisted Pete, quite at a loss to keep an important conversation going as he waved her spoon away.

Carolyn served herself, leaving Pete to recover a little.

'I meant it to happen,' she neatly said, and began to eat. Peter only had time to open his mouth before she continued.

'It's best for the three of us. You've got two and I'll have one. You live your life and I'll live mine. Jeff'll see sense. I've waited five years, Pete, and it's not worked with Jeff. He'll come round. It's the only way.'

Carolyn's common sense floored Pete completely.

'But it's my child. You can't just take my child,' he said, and sat back in his chair with no thought of eating or drinking.

'You can't take me, Pete. See reason. You need your good job, you've got the house and the family. It's good.'

'No, it isn't, it isn't at all', repeated Pete. He'd never told Carolyn about Steph's neglect of Peter, the head banging cot boy or his new worries about Helen. No-one but he knew about Carolyn, the caring woman in his life, and now even she wasn't making much sense to him.

'Jeff'll never believe it's his,' he followed up. 'He can't love a child which isn't his own.'

'I know him, Pete. He will, because he's seen me gawping in all the Baby shops. He can't do what he can't do. You know what I mean.'

'You seem so sure. It can't be true he'd accept it just like that, if you're supposed to have been going to Granny for a special purpose he seems to have known about?' Pete's incredulity was real.

'He's not a stupid man, he's a kind one. You're the good one.' Carolyn leaned over to kiss Pete on the cheek. 'Eat up because it's got to be tonight we let him know.'

They both cleared up after the meal, then Pete drove behind Carolyn's car to her home twenty minutes away. He was to sit down in the kitchen while Carolyn spoke to Jeff.

It was a bright, tidy, square room with a pantry off. Pete could see Carolyn's steady hands at work in here. There would be more paraphernalia to tidy away, a reassuring mother to hang out the nappies and a larder stocked with weaning food. He didn't feel used, but he did feel cheated, until he saw Jeff's face as he came in the door.

Pete kicked the table leg awkwardly as he got up to shake an outstretched hand, then sat down again abruptly. He couldn't take in the man. He just felt sorry, suddenly, for all kids in cots.

'She's told me everything,' said Jeff and sat down himself. He was a tall man. He didn't sit down wearily. It just took a few seconds longer to get his legs under the table it seemed.

'We're going to work it out between us. I just want Carolyn to be happy.'

Peter turned from a loved woman and the prospect of a loved child, and set off for his mother's house. In all the pandemonium of early morning with two babies and Steph lying in bed, he caught up with Elsie in the kitchen. He'd known it all his life. Small, like a lobby into the garden, he felt cramped and awkward in it as he spoke.

'I'd leave Steph, Mum, but she'd just plonk herself and the two of them on you. I can't control what she does any more, can I? Mothers are supposed to love their kids. How's she been getting on with Helen?' Pete needed to know honestly as Elsie saw the look on his face.

'Oh, it's been on and off, you know. Some days she has her wits about her, others it's fags and mags and I can't get her to see to anything, yet she's not stupid, Pete.' Elsie was blunt and considerate, but, like her son who had made the wrong choice on a fateful day in this same kitchen, she was as incredulous as he was at the turn of events. 'I'd have them here, but I can't all the time. It takes it out of me,' she continued. 'I'll have them as often as you need them to come.'

'No, Mum, thanks,' said Pete, and they both heard Helen wake up. 'I'll sort it at my end. I'm going to give us a chance as a foursome. I'll arrange babysitters so Helen gets a life. If I take Steph out more she might wake up to things.'

'But what about your job?' Elsie spoke up for her son. His work for the Government was a source of pride and the early death of her husband a few years before made that a strength for her.

'I'll get by on some better shifts,' said Pete, defensively. 'I'll do my best.' He got up. 'I'll get Helen. Steph won't.'

Elsie didn't have a visit for another year. 'Phone calls gave her indications. Steph was good with postcards. They'd got out and about to local resorts that summer and a cheery line or two about her grandchildren was all she received.

Then came news of a third child on the way. Elsie knew that the game was up for Pete. If a child was to save a marriage this was going the wrong way about it. She'd been in the same position with an argumentative husband when son number three was meant to keep the genie in the bottle. It did no such thing. Genies have venomous tongues and a sting in their vaporous tail. Of course she loved her three boys all under ten, and not too much of a handful at the beginning. She did her very best by them, but the constant arguments reverberated around the small house even after her husband's death. What did the boys hear? What did the boys know?

In the West country, Pete took the news badly.

'You've done this deliberately to keep me tied, Steph. I know you have. You've made it so hard for Peter and then Helen. You can't look after kids. You haven't got it in you!' he shouted at her.

'I'm looking after Peter and Helen,' Steph raised her voice in reply. 'I'm here all the time, aren't I?'

God knows I don't get out, and as to knowing what you get up to out there in your big, wide, secret world, well, I'm in the know, I don't think.' She turned to light up a cigarette. 'I'm here for them all, you can see that for yourself.'

'I don't see a pretty picture, Steph. If you don't make out good with this one, I'll be off,' said Pete as cigarette smoke drifted towards him.

'Oh, yes, and who'll be with you? Someone from the Secret Service?' Steph openly sneered at his job.

'I'd make sure you never knew, just like the job,' he said as he went out of the room.

Janet was a quiet baby, born in the local Hospital. Steph had to make arrangements for Peter and Helen to be minded, as Pete could not get time off. Mandy brought three year old Peter and fifteen month old pretty Helen to see baby Janet.

'I got them both ready,' she said. 'They were fine,' and then her smile stopped. 'I found a lot of things to deal with. Has your washing machine been on the blink, Steph? There was hardly a clean towel, sheet or pillowcase in the whole house.'

'It's not been the easiest time to deal with things', replied Steph. 'It was good of you to take the trouble.'

'I can always come round, you know that. These two are just lovely to be with and your new one looks a sweetie,' said Mandy.

'I'll be fine when I get settled back,' said Steph, then, 'Do you like the name we've given her?' She sat up in the hospital bed holding her third child.

Elsie saw Janet that same Christmas and New Year. The two girls were pretty with their dark eyes together looking brightly at the woman they hardly knew. Peter was more voluble. He'd got an aeroplane from Father Christmas.

'Nana, look. I can make it fly,' he called to her.

'In fact, it was Pete who was aiming to be off.

'There's no change, Mum,' he said at one breakfast. 'You can see how long she spends in bed here. She just lights up and reads until the screams and pleads make her move. I'm not there often to see it, but the state of the house says it all. Her excuses are empty now, Mum. She can't hide any longer and I'm getting a divorce on the grounds of parental neglect. I've been offered a fantastic job in Television in South Africa. I'm going to take it.'

Elsie sighed. 'It's your life, Pete. I'll do my best this end if that's what you want.'

'No, Mum,' Pete said firmly. 'We'll both leave her to it. I've got things arranged.'

'What sort of things?' asked Elsie.

'You'll see,' he replied.

Soon Elsie heard the tale. Towards Easter it was. Steph wrote a full letter. It arrived crumpled and dated the week before.

'…..Pete's going to send me money from his swanky new job in Johannesburg, but he's pulled the plug on everything else. Social Services came yesterday to take Helen and Janet into care. They explained my legal position. I've still got Peter here and he'll be checked weekly.

I can't help it if it's all gone wrong. There's been too much secrecy in Pete's job for him to open up with me. He could have helped a lot more without that, but don't get me wrong, I want you to come for Easter or Whit if you can. I get to have the girls back for the Bank Holidays.

Come down and see us. These three are all you've got of him now. We're none of us likely to see Pete again.'

All my love,

Steph

# Conversing Skills

It was just before closing on a Tuesday afternoon.

'It'll be a fiver to you,' said Laurie. 'I've seen you before.'

'Laurie, I've done more than seen you in here. I've bought you quite a few drinks,' replied Martin. 'I won't give you a fiver, you numbskull, it's worth a lot more, but I'll run to a tenner.' Martin opened the pub till.

'Thanks, mate,' said Laurie and took the note in exchange for a canvas he'd finished painting that week. He handed it over the bar.

'It's fantastic! How do you do it, Laurie?' Martin leaned from the stool behind the bar of the pub, 'The Bushel and Peck,' with one elbow, resting the painting horizontally on his knees. He had to open them wide.

'Doesn't really need a frame does it?' he quizzed Laurie.

Laurie shrugged. 'Can't make out what might suit best. It's up to you how you do it.'

'Well, the missus always likes what I buy of yours. It's beer and paint for you, then?'

'Something like that,' murmured Laurie.

'How old are you now, Laurie?' said Martin as Laurie looked like he'd stay after the transaction. 'I see you're looking at Babs some evenings and she's no spring chicken. She's been by most nights since her kids have grown up a bit.'

'Well, you might run the pub, but you don't own everyone in it,' said Laurie, looking as if he might move off the stool. He'd only just sat down.

'Hang on, Laurie, you know I didn't mean it like that. What'll you have, on me?' He squared up to his most unusual customer.

'Just a pint, thanks,' came the reply.

'Any luck with that job we spoke about last week?' said Martin.

'It didn't go anywhere, but anyway it wouldn't have made up for that good job I lost where I was groundsman. They got in new machinery and dumped me quick as they could. I did a good job. I'm just thirty, for God's sake!' Laurie took the free beer and jumped it a step on the glass counter.

'So, now you're painting, and where did you get that from in your blood?' asked Martin curiously.

'Don't know really. My brother got me started on classes but I didn't like what they said, so I stopped listening. It was like school, I did the same there. What was the point of going?' Laurie hunched up over the single pint.

'You might have learned a bit if you'd stayed,' said Martin encouragingly, 'but you seem to know enough now. That's why I said, where does it come from, and you don't know?'

'My mum's older sister did a bit of painting, only carrying on from painting by numbers at home. She worked in a craft shop and she was good with her hands.' Laurie replied.

'The beer's got you going, Laurie. Anyone else, like someone famous?' smiled Martin.

'Well, what's famous?' said Laurie smartly. 'I've looked at lots of pictures in books my brother got me from the Library and I've copied a few of them. I'm sure it was you who had that small Degas, the ballet girls I did, wasn't it?'

'Yes, that was me,' replied Martin, 'and it's in our lounge now. It's good, Laurie, it's good. You should take your work more seriously and get it out there.'

'Where's out there?' Laurie almost growled. 'Out there treats you badly. Out there's got funny customers. I like people I know. Babs wants me to paint more and 'get out there', but what's the point?' Halfway down his beer glass, he'd really found his tongue. 'I know what I like doing and it isn't pleasing other people. I do what I need to do in my paintings.'

Martin paused slightly at this flow, quite taken aback.

'But, you're good.' Martin foundered for the words. 'Your technique must be as good as anyone's up at the local Gallery and probably some in London, if you'd admit it.'

'I can't be sure of that, though. My brother buys me the stuff, 'specially the acrylic paints. They don't come cheap. I'd do a landscape for him and his wife, but I don't, I like the other sort I paint,' said Laurie, now more relaxed and looking up at Martin.

'You know that one of the three witches you did, Laurie? It had no background. It was like the three were in full close up, right under a magnifying glass. You even painted their muscles bulging and every ugly hair on their big, ugly faces. Who paints like that?' Martin was becoming keen on answers.

'I don't mind ugliness,' said Laurie, looking down. 'You can't tell me there isn't enough of that to go round.'

'True,' replied Martin, 'but if you paint pictures, they are supposed to lighten up a room, not make people try to leave. You made that picture spooky enough. Mind you, John, he liked it.'

'Yes, he would,' murmured Laurie, reminded of a hail-fellow-well-met type about six months ago.

'How much did you let him have that one for then?' said Martin, who was getting more than a pint's worth from Laurie today. He broadened his smile at the answer.

'He gave me a whopping twenty five quid, which isn't a bad price for three ugly mugs.' Laurie's face lightened at the memory.

'Ridiculous price, and you know it,' said Martin, aiming to prod hard. 'If that was a work of genius, and it might be, because I've never seen anything like it, then he'll be the first to flog it in London and make a mint.'

'Lucky him, then,' responded the artist. 'Who's to say what genius is? When I'm painting, I'm painting. I'm not trying to be a genius. Still, I don't want to mess it up either. Everything's so expensive in art.'

Martin began to shift on his bar chair. Laurie sat impassive.

'Genius is about ideas,' Martin said. 'How on earth do you get your ideas?' He really thought that this question would make Laurie tell him a thing or two.

'Ideas come from the back of you through the brush, or when I get my pencil out. They're not there when I get the new canvas my brother's just bought me. They seem to be there in the tip of the pencil. Sometimes my best new idea comes when a colour goes wrong. Instead of getting me angry, it moves me on.' Laurie skated his empty glass across the bar.

'It'll be time for me to move on, I don't doubt,' he said, and looked solemnly at Martin. 'Don't you make any remark about me to Babs, okay? My next picture is a big one, for her. She likes one of the stories I like, so I'm going to have a go at the main character. You might get to see it, you might not.' Laurie got up, but didn't move off.

'Oh, and who's that character then?' said Martin quickly. 'Bet he's never been in this pub.'

'No, but you must have met a few like him,' Laurie laughed lightly. 'It's Scrooge. I'm painting him with Marley's ghost. I even remember that bit being read to me at school.'

'So that's a lot of white paint then?' smiled Martin.

'No, he won't look like a boiled egg with black eyes, I'm giving him a bit of a watery presence, more green than grey and more yellow than white.' Laurie realised what he had said when Martin made a face at him and followed with, 'She won't vomit on it!'

'I should think not,' said Martin, 'but you'll give it to her, not sell it, you say? It's just that I don't want you done down, you know that Laurie. We'd all rather have you in here happy than up town kicking your heels, but your canvasses ought to go a good deal further than this bar.' Martin spoke firmly as Laurie turned his tall frame away.

'You've got that one now, so what more do you want?' said Laurie, seemingly finding it difficult to go.

'Art work isn't a question of owning something, Laurie, it's about knowing what you've got. Thanks to you I've got a bargain, but with your talent you should get the lion's share.' Martin shook a finger at Laurie. 'You know I'm right, you know you do.'

'You're talking just like my brother. He's always pushing me into projects, new ways to get me involved.' Laurie raised his voice imperceptibly and turned back to the bar edge. 'I just don't want other people's ideas. I want my own in paint. It doesn't matter what I paint. The idea is in the painted head or the arm or the hand. When I get the hang of it, it'll be in any tree I paint, too. I get the idea, then the paint takes over.'

'You mean you're moving into landscapes? They'd sell well, Laurie,' said Martin.

'No, I don't exactly mean that. I don't want to paint fields and hills and trees, I want to paint the ideas in them. Every tree is different for different's sake.'

Laurie leaned on the bar. He looked like a tree himself in a way. He was tall and very thin with wavy brown hair curling up at all angles over his head.

'You paint me a landscape for twenty five quid, then,' said Martin with a wry smile. 'How about the view outside my pub? It's got the roundabout. It's got that tree on it and the road opposite goes down to the river. What could you make of that?'

'I'll tell you what I'd make of it,' said Laurie and he shook his head at every punctuating point. 'I'd draw the stupid roundabout like it caged the tree. I'd draw the stupid tree like it held up the sky. I'd paint the stupid tarmac like there was hell underneath and you'd never hang something like that behind your bar.'

Martin stepped back.

'Now then, I'd buy anything of yours because your prices are good and you don't get far to sell them. The missus likes the light you've caught in the ones we've got.'

Laurie took a deep breath saying, 'I'm glad about that then. Tell you what, let your wife tell me what she'd like me to paint. Perhaps she'd get me a pretty box of chocolates and I'd paint what's on the lid.'

Martin refused to be drawn on that one. Wives don't generally count in art.

"Course not,' he said. 'When I said 'brighten up the room', I meant it brightens her up because it's in the room. All paintings have got to hang in a room, haven't they?'

'I'd like mine to cover one wall, or maybe one wall and the one beside it, like a corner doesn't exist. And what about on a ceiling? There's plenty of artists who had stiff necks.' Laurie was smiling at Martin now, none too keen to let go by a free beer on his next visit.

'You could paint me a mural behind the bar, then. I'd move all the shelving and you'd have a blank canvas,' said Martin, returning Laurie's smile.

'Well, I'd do a bit better than vineyards, grapes and olives like the pub chains,' said Laurie. 'Have you seen that one in the town, the 'White Horse? It's like Italy with no Italians,' said Laurie scathingly.

'They put them up like rolls of wallpaper, and it takes about half an hour they say.' Martin turned to his short length of bar wall.

'The themed ones are the worst, don't you think? In town they've got 'The Pilgrim's Progress' and their murals show a bloke with a great sack on his back. He's going nowhere very fast. It right cheers you up. If you gave me the chance I'd paint cloud and mist on mountain after crazy mountain going into the distance. There wouldn't be any roads going up. There'd be no way up,' he said by way of conclusion.

'That'd put the customers off,' said Martin. 'They all drink until they're in cloud cuckoo land as it is and I suppose everyone's got a different sort of cuckoo land. Maybe you ought to paint in the way down, the way they'd feel tomorrow if they drank too much,' he laughed. 'That man, Dante, didn't he get some painter to paint that in red and black with a few flames?'

'Yes,' said Laurie as he did turn to leave the pub, 'One hell too many for me then.'

Martin began to wipe the bar.

'Cheers, mate.'

# Two's a crowd

Ellen read the embroidered postcard again. 'Give all my love to the two darling girls,' her husband, Bob, had written from France. It was May 1917 and Iris was already four years old and older sister, Irene, six, was home from school and telling her sister all about it in the hallway.

'We all got a nice, new sharpened pencil, today. Our crayon tray has only got reds, browns and oranges in it, so Miss Mountford is getting in greens and blues. I'm going to draw a river like the one in the Park,' said Irene to her sister, who was sitting on her bottom in the narrow hall. As Iris sat there, her flounced pinafore spread out around her ankles. The ankles were covered by soft, white socks, and the feet by black leather single bar buttoned shoes which her mother had put on for the short walk to Irene's school to fetch her. It was four o'clock in the afternoon and the very worst time of the day. The girls would argue all the way to bedtime.

Ellen put down the carefully sent card, quickly breathed a prayer for Bob at the Front and went through to collect her daughters in the hallway.

'Iris,' she said, unpinning her hat as she spoke, 'you can get up now.'

The afternoon light from the two glass panes in the door shone onto the girls' heads. Irene's curly dark hair hung down all over her shoulders from under the small felt hat. It was tousled from a day at school but still shone from the morning's brushing. Iris's hair was thin, straight and lacklustre and never caught the light at all. Ellen looked at Iris, whose hat had been pushed onto one side by contact with the wall and sighed again at the wide righthand parting over a high forehead, making her look like a doll with an unfinished hair line. Ellen had brushed and brushed it into thickness, forward, back and to each side morning after morning, but the hair would not grow over the space. Irene's thick hair fell fully over her face and into her eyes, there was so much of it. Like the hair, little Iris was hard work for her mother.

At her mother's voice, Iris reacted just as Ellen thought she would. She had about half a dozen naughty ploys at the moment and across her bright blue, wide eyes all six came into view for choice it seemed. Ellen received this one.

'I won't, until you let me have a biscuit with my milk,' she said to the chest where her chin rested.

'Well, Iris, if you had been good this morning, you could have had two biscuits, but you weren't, you know you weren't.'

Iris had cried all the way back home from taking Irene to School. She'd hung onto every lamp- post in the short journey, twisting round them like a dervish and quite determined to become dizzy.

'I want to go to school, too,' she cried out over and over again.

'You'll be able to go next year, Iris. Daddy is going to be home for a fortnight to see you go to school and be a big girl.' Ellen had patiently waited for the tantrum to pass, holding out her hand for Iris to take it obediently. Iris had slapped her mother's hand down.

'I want to be a big girl now,' Iris had said, then, 'I can be,' and had swung round and round on the lamp post until Ellen worried for her right arm. Then the left shoe strap had broken with the jerking movement of the swinging and the stepping up and down the pavement. Ellen could see it flapping over Iris's foot.

'Come on now, Iris,' said Ellen firmly. 'Look what you've done to your shoe.' She took hold of her daughter by the arm and took off the broken shoe with a quick lunge, bending down. Iris had to walk home hobbledehoy with one shoe and a stockinged foot. It was not the same sort of game as turning round the lamp posts, and her cries went up to another level. Ellen's hold of her daughter didn't slacken. How she wished Bob had the other hand of the child, lifting her up like a swing along the road just as if it had been in the park. Bob had done this with her daily on his last leave. Irene had grumbled, but she got all the cuddles afterwards. Being the older girl she'd always seen a lot more of her father.

When Ellen and Iris arrived at their home, a terraced brick house in a quiet side road, Iris's cries began to abate. Even the little girl realised how much louder her cries seemed in the neatly empty road. The family of four rented number fifteen. It was about halfway down looking no more distinctive than its neighbours. Each house had a mere yard of a front walled garden and some had a wide hedge up to the window sill, almost denying that there was a patch of brown earth altogether. Each house joined at the doorway had its own alleyway with an arched entrance leading down to a garden gate right or left, so you knew your neighbour at the door for the milkman and your neighbour at the garden gate for the coalman who came to the back. Tidy, respectable and with not too high a rent, Bob and Ellen had moved in seven years ago when they married. The two girls came along but then came the War, taking Bob from his job as a mechanic in the local Garage where he serviced businessmen's cars to become an Ambulance driver at the Front. Every day had been a worry to Ellen since then.

Now the two girls were in the narrow hallway of their home, ready for another autumn evening of dispute and bickering.

'I'll have one biscuit then, won't I, Mummy?' said Iris.

'Yes, it'll be milk and a biscuit for each of you,' replied Ellen and immediately saw Irene's face fall.

'But I can have two, Mummy, because Iris has been naughty. I ought to have two. I've been good at school today,' she said and gave her sister a kick with her foot as Iris sat in the hallway blocking her way forward.

'Get up Iris, so we can all get on,' said Ellen.

Iris turned her body over so that she lay with her tummy on the lino hall covering. She banged with her two fists on the wall of the hallway and drummed her feet up and down at the same time.

'I want two biscuits, too. Two biscuits, too,' she chanted as she thumped.

Ellen's head was beginning to ache. She helped Irene step over her sister so that she could go to the kitchen and wait for her milk and biscuit.

'Get up at once, Iris,' she said when Irene had stepped by. 'Tomorrow we are going to the Photographers in town so we can send a picture to daddy in France.'

'I won't go,' shouted Iris as she got up and slapped her mother on the hand again, the second time that day.

'That's enough from you for one day,' said Ellen in a quiet fury with the younger daughter who was so different to the first. 'For that, you're going to the coal hole.'

Ellen took hold of Iris around her determinedly broad waist and pushed her in front of her to the door of the kitchen, not to follow Irene for after-school milk and biscuits, but to propel her past a smiling Irene to the back door and out into the small paved yard. There a brick lean-to had two doors, one the outside toilet and the other the cavernous cupboard for the coal.

Iris screamed all the more until she was put inside. The door was shut and locked and the screams died down to whimpering cries.

Ellen went back to the kitchen, gave Irene her milk and two biscuits, but didn't sit with her. She went instead to the front room to sit with the photos of her husband and to re-read the postcards.

News came just over a year later, just before Christmas 1918 when Ellen had been hoping to have her husband home at the end of the War, that Bob Smythe had died in the Influenza epidemic sweeping Europe. He had survived the duration of the War but was caught out, like millions, by the dreaded disease.

That Christmas holiday, Ellen took the two girls to her Northamptonshire parents. The house in the small town was similar to their own. In the warm kitchen with its range, the seven and five year old granddaughters sat at a small table, colouring in a drawing for Nana. The crayons were a Christmas present and had a good range of colours for Irene's artistic eye. Iris was determined to break each crayon into two.

'Don't do that, Iris,' said Nana as she saw Iris look at the crayons and her small movement forward. 'We'll share the colours without breaking them.'

'I just wanted blue and Irene's got it,' said Iris.

'Well, get on with another colour while you wait for your sister to finish,' reasoned Nana and she put her hand on the table to emphasise her point. Iris picked up a yellow for the sun.

In the back room, where French doors led out onto a well-swept area of paving, Ellen and grandpa looked out into the small garden.

'While you're here, Ellen, can we have a photo taken of the girls? There's a 'bus into Northampton at nine tomorrow. We'll get dressed up for Thomas's on the High Street,' said her father.

'Yes, of course,' said Ellen, 'I packed their best dresses.'

'Of course you did. That's just like you to please us,' said Grandpa.

'I always did to please Bob,' said Ellen and turned her face away. Her father watched her as she roamed the small room in her black dress.

'How will I manage, dad, until the War Widows' Pension comes?' said Ellen. 'Other women in the street had to wait a while. Mrs. Johnson lost her husband three years ago.'

'You'll have to get in a lodger, Ellen. Find a widow like yourself, or a spinster. Ask the Vicar for a bit of help in that,' he replied.

Ellen turned, her face further saddened by the thought of more sorrow in the house.

'It's Iris, really. She's so very naughty at home. I suppose she's better now she's at school, but any lodger will want a quiet house,' said Ellen.

'She'll change. She loved her doll and the pram this Christmas, didn't she? She'll want to get back to play with it and then get to school. See the New Year as a new beginning if you can, dear,' was his sympathetic reply.

And 1919 came. It's very date irked Ellen all year. At nineteen she'd met Bob, at nineteen. A nineteen year old lady's maid who met a dashing chauffeur up at Stornay for the Shoot. Eight years married, two girls and Bob dead at only thirty years old.

Iris always asked about her daddy at bedtime. Irene was pertinent this year. She was getting on well in lessons and liked to make Iris, now that she was at school, feel she was the youngest and the worst.

'I don't draw trees like that, Iris. Yours looks like a lollipop on a stick, doesn't it?' she said, leaning over her sister and pointing out the clumsy blob of green.

'Trees are that colour, aren't they, mummy?' came the bewildered reply from Iris, unaware of any definition at her age.

'Of course they are, Iris. Irene meant that they have branches, like arms, so they spread out a bit,' said her mother kindly.

Irene always poked fun at her sister, finding her funny in all the wrong ways. Even that photograph with the doll's pram which well-meaning neighbours had taken in the New Year showed Irene with the pram hood up to the camera so that the doll could not be seen. Iris arranged her doll to be quite upright and looking at it. She then looked fondly at the doll's wide face, but Irene looked at the camera almost as contemptuous of it as of the hidden doll.

As the year went on, the differences between the girls widened perceptibly. Irene blossomed with all the attention at school and then expected praise at home. Iris began to prefer home to school and snuffled her way to being kept off as well as achieving little in her first year there. Worst of all was the end of November when it was Iris's birthday close to the anniversary of Bob's death in France just before Christmas. A whole month before her birthday, not unlike other children of her age, Iris lived the anticipation.

'What have I got for my birthday? Have you bought it? Can I have it?' she managed to squeal in some form or another for almost all of October. Irene sneered at her eagerness.

'Can't you keep quiet about your birthday? Miss Hill says, 'those who say before the day, keep the cakes and gifts away', so there!' She had made it all up, but it sounded sinister to Iris, whose impatience for the big day knew no bounds.

Ellen opened the front door on a Saturday before the Wednesday birthday and found a neighbour with a nicely wrapped parcel for Iris to save for the big day. Iris ran up from the kitchen, thinking it was the postman.

'It's mine, isn't it?' she said loudly from behind her mother's skirts, and then she jumped forward, snatched the parcel from the hands of an astonished Mrs. Beamish and sat down on the hall mat to tear it open there and then.

'Iris, stop that!' cried her mother in shame and desperation. 'It isn't your birthday yet. You've got to give it to me for later.' She tried to take the present from Iris, but she was too late. A book and a skipping rope saw the light of day and Iris's eyes gleamed brightly. She clutched them both and looked up at Mrs. Beamish.

'These are nice. It's my birthday, isn't it?' and so saying she pushed by her mother and ran to the kitchen.

'I'm so sorry, Ada,' said Ellen. 'It's her age, I think. Thank you very much for thinking of her,' and she closed the door on her friend.

Ellen walked down the short, dark passage, entered the small kitchen and saw Irene drawing at the table. She looked unusually conscientious. Going out by the back door and into the cramped back yard, she found soon to be seven year old Iris skipping in a cold wind.

Just as she was about to speak, she saw a streak of red on the girl's pinafore. It was blood from a bad scratch on the hand which was trying to twirl the rope.

'How did that happen?' she said as she firmly stopped her daughter skipping. 'Look how naughty you've been and look what you've done.'

'Irene did it,' said Iris, stopping jerkily and stepping back. 'She scratched me with her fingernails when I showed her my presents.'

'That's because you shouldn't have your presents yet, Iris,' said Ellen with a worried smile. 'Come in. We'll wash that and I'll ask Irene what she did to you.'

Two daughters missed a punishment that day, but only because it was November 1919.

Irene won a scholarship at eleven years and it was just about within the means of Ellen's budget to provide the uniform and the shoes which were required. There were gym shoes, ballet shoes, walking to school shoes, hockey boots and tennis whites. Ellen dispensed with a front room and took in another lodger from the time of Irene's increased expense. She walked with a tray of photos into the back room parlour and placed them as nicely as she could on the crowded upright piano. She'd got a single spring bed from her friend, Ada, and spoke to her about the girls.

'Irene's done well, but at a price, Ada,' she said with a sigh. 'She's a very grown-up twelve year old, but Iris doesn't seem to grow up at all. It's her birthday coming up again and you know what she's like.' Ellen smiled ruefully and poured the tea in the back parlour. 'I only managed the uniform at the beginning of the term and soon it'll be presents again and again.'

'We're lucky to be in this road, though, Ellen. Everyone helps out, like they did for the War Memorial last year,' said Ada.

Ellen stood up to fetch the frame with that very photograph in. In it, Ellen stood with Ada, Phyllis and Dorothy, three of her friends, and with three other ladies of the Parish who had helped to raise funds for the memorial.

'Oh yes,' said Ada, frowning. 'I wouldn't wear that big a hat now.'

'No, you wouldn't,' laughed Ellen as she replaced the frame.

Almost all of the photos of the two girls growing up during the War had been taken especially to send to Bob in France. Now, it was just for occasions and Ellen wanted a photo to mark Irene's first term at the Grammar School and Iris's tenth birthday in the November. She bought the two girls identical cream pinafore-front dresses from the department store in the town. They were in a coarse weave cotton with a lace motif cut in at the neckline. The sleeves were three quarter and the hem ended at the knee. Black stockings, black shoes and a white headband for each girl completed the picture. Irene was so much taller than Iris now that she looked nearly fifteen. Iris still looked a little dumpy, neither grown outwards or upwards, but together they looked the picture of happiness.

'I don't want my hair down over my shoulders, Mummy,' said Iris as she looked in the mirror that day.

'I want you both to look the same,' said Ellen. 'That's why I bought the dresses. Stand still while I curl up your hair, Iris.'

'At least mine doesn't need the curlers,' said Irene as she brushed by her sister, sitting with her mother on the girls' bed. 'One job less, Mummy.'

'You make lots of jobs for Mummy,' said Iris, trying not to be burned by the curling tongs. 'Mummy is always at the shops for your school things.'

'I don't mind that, Iris. I shop for your birthday, too,' ventured Ellen, hoping not to unleash a tirade of 'want, want, want!' from Iris.

'Well,' said Irene, bumping down on a chair. 'Which do you want us to wear round our necks, Mummy? Can I have the locket and Iris the pearls?'

Iris grimaced. 'I wanted the locket this time,' she said. 'You had it last time, when we were with Nana.'

The two girls did not have very many trinkets and they shared several necklaces given them by their grandparents

'This isn't the time to argue,' said Ellen firmly, uncurling the tongs from near Iris's wide parting, 'or I'll never get this right.'

On the 'bus into town, Iris looked as if she'd settle to the arrangement, Ellen thought, but Irene was quiet and withdrawn.

They knew Blake and Edgar's Photographers very well. This time, the girls looked so grown that Tom Edgar said in his front shop.

'Well, Mrs. Smythe, this'll be good. You must be proud.'

He didn't say much, but it was enough for Ellen.

At the rear of the shop was the studio where the girls felt at home. They had been quite often and were one of many fatherless families in the town who were customers of Mr. Edgar. The girls were to sit on a white wooden bench for two. It looked like an upturned bookcase with its straight arms. Iris was asked to sit sidesaddle at the back, Irene with her long legs in black stockings sat on the front, the two of them entwined as you might in a love seat. The photographer asked them both to look down at an open book on Irene's lap. He achieved a perfect heart shape in composition from the curve of the girls' heads over to the crossed

45

point of Irene's shoes. The new dresses were on show, the hair hung in curls, the girls smiled.

From this point on Irene kept herself busy with studies. Iris did not follow her sister to Grammar School and made up for her lack of homework by playing with friends in the street who were never friends with Irene, bookish and shut in the home. Later, as a secretary in the town, her circle was wider and the two young ladies met young men with cameras who took much less restrained photographs. They snapped their independence of one another and of mother. The swing of a floral dress and the raising of a bared arm showed both the defiance of the early Thirties and their freedom as the current beau aimed the Brownie at them.

To Ellen's astonishment, Colin called one day to ask for Iris's hand. He had the ring.

'You lucky girl,' said Ellen, when he had gone. 'He's such a nice young man.'

Iris was just coming out from her small bedroom.

'Irene's Nigel seems keen. She's not so fond of him, do you think, Iris?' she continued.

'I don't know, Mum,' said Iris, but not without humour. 'She can have who she likes with all that hair and her blue eyes, but she's so hard to please. She's thinking of turning him down for Will. She'll be hoping he'll propose quickly now.'

Ellen smiled too. 'It's you with your bobbed hair that got the man, is it then, Iris? I didn't think that when you persuaded me to let it be cut when you were fifteen.'

'Well, I'm nineteen now, Mum, and Colin likes it this way,' said Iris.

They both heard Irene come in downstairs. She always turned the key in the lock with an irritable jerk of the wrist.

A few months later, Ethel looked in the mirror at the grey hair curling around her face. Her photo of Bob in the highland kilt taken in Stornoway for her was on the dressing table. He was full of life then, just like Colin. The letter that morning to say that he had died of Tuberculosis had sent Iris to her room to sob as Ellen had never heard her in all her tantrum days. The small bedroom echoed horribly with gurgling cries of loss, frustration, tenderness and fear. Ellen could scarcely believe that her wilful daughter had been courted by and engaged to a young man of such prospects. With her father's zest for life, Iris had received the worst blow of all.

Irene's marriage quite soon after to a labouring man after rebuffing Nigel, the 'good catch', was not a subject to bring up with her elder daughter, who was evidently determined to be married first as a right. Then Iris seemed unhappily eager to be married alongside. Her enthusiasm for Gerald was overstated and outsized. Ellen considered both her daughters to be marrying the wrong men for different reasons; Irene to get her own way, Iris to open the next present when the first had been so soon broken.

They both wore lockets at their weddings. Ethel had bought them one each for their day. Iris never showed hers to anyone and only half a century later did the grandchildren find the tiniest photos of herself and Colin, cut with jerking nail scissors to the small heart shapes. Irene's locket was tidily empty. And so it was that both young women began their married lives with men they hardly loved. In one wedding photo, Ellen came behind the two couples, diminished in size by age and uncertain where to place herself, there being no Bob to stand the other side. The photographer snapped her asymmetrically, peering between Will and Irene, but she knew it was the habit of both her daughters to find even two too much of a crowd.

# Caught in the Light

His mother sat scribbling in a notebook. She was going to give a talk on liberal schooling and usually spoke of her two sons as examples of the system under which they had studied. Johann had achieved, Anton had failed. It could hardly be fairer than that; that she calculated from a humanist perspective. The brothers had been given names to reflect the family's diverse European past.

'Mug of tea?' asked Johann, but his backpack was already hoisted onto his back.

'No thanks, Johann,' said Shirley. 'Anton will get me one later when he comes down.'

Anton and Johann had been brought up in their large house, 'Warren Edge', and had their entire education in the Sussex countryside. It had been set up in the post First World War decade by those anxious to renew and do something to recoup loss. The peace of the surrounding countryside was paramount. The ancient woodland and weald rose up, a challenge and a divide, but for the smaller children there was a slope to call an adventure and a suntrap for outdoor lessons.

Johann went out into the garden, making for the gate. His mother knew exactly where he was going. He wasn't at home often, but when he was, he walked. Tall and thin for his almost mid-twenties, Johann probably did look studious. There was s slight bend to the head, an imperceptibly slower than usual walk and a gaze that tried to sum up and make a subtraction at the same time.

Johann was deliberating on actions, which very uncomfortably, a weekend before, he had found to speak much louder than words. He had not told his parents, nor would he confide in Anton. Anton would have wowed and whooped about the garden mimicking the actions of the tale to impress his older brother. A diagnosis when he was twenty had led to a considerable change of lifestyle. He helped at home in the large garden between hospital stays and adjustments to medication.

Johann turned into a leafy lane and covered a lot of dappled shade with his long stride. Arching overhead with leaf buds only just broken in the March sunshine, White Poplar moved gently in an upper breeze. He'd learned to look up at an early age. Green sunlight of a kind chlorophyll might purchase for itself if it wasn't freely available, streamed from a blue-white sky. At the end of the lane there was a pond and a seat looking like journey's end. He sat down on the bench and swung his legs onto the wooden slats to measure leg to log and leaned back on rounded corner post.

Who was there to share his thoughts and his story? He looked down into the pond.

'Come on, Johann. You can't sit and just watch the moat. We want to get on it!' said Nicola, who didn't do much more than speak her mind most of the time. Her father owned the old house, its moated environs and large parkland as a business venture. Nicola's undergraduate friends were there for a weekend and she was determined to make it a memorable, moonlit one.

'I don't mind joining you, Johann,' said Russell, who was second year at the same College, 'but it'll be cold after sundown. Just look at the sky.'

Nicola turned to her boyfriend, Peter.

I'll get Nat and Daniel. They'll help us bring round the punt I used when I was a kid.'

As the boat party left, laughing and skipping up and down the sloping grassy bank of the moat, Johann beckoned Russell to sit down.

'This is better than Oxford,' he said with a smile. 'Soon we'll have a punt of our own, no tourists and nothing to pay.'

'Good of Nicola, isn't it?' replied Russell. 'It's Peter's idea to get all his friends together for a jolly. I didn't realise that the place was so old.'

'It's a lot older than me. Even so, I'm ahead of you lot by about five years. I wonder if that confers anything?' said Johann.

'Only if your Tutor thinks your Thesis confers anything on him.' laughed Russell. 'He'll bask in your glory. Don't they all?'

'I'll complete at the end of this year. It'll be due at the end of August, then I'll get post-doctoral work.'

'Well then, we'll see you here more often. Nicola wants to make this a regular fixture, doubtless to string Peter along.' Russell got up as he spoke.

'Going in?' said Johann.

The soft red brick of the Tudor building was mellowed to peach in the lowered February sunlight. Nicola had said that a fire had been laid in the Great Hall, which must be the centre of the E-shape. They found steps up to a kitchen door, then a corridor to work their way around to the grand rooms.

They found the lofty room lit as it had been for centuries by a dimming sunlight and the glow of a log fire. A long oak trestle table lay along the window side and another squarer table took up almost all of the rest of the space in the room with high-backed chairs around it. Sideboards stood at each end, flanking the doors.

'No easy chairs here, Johann. Let's go through and see what we can find. They won't miss us in the punt,' said Russell.

Johann led the way through a darkened hallway to a room as large as the dining room but its furnishing spoke of comfort rather than grandeur.

Russell rushed to the squidgiest of the old armchairs. His brown jumper and corduroys matched the leather almost exactly.

'This is more like it. We'll eat in the other place when we get Nicola back and find the kitchen. Anyone can fix us a pizza or two.'

He sank down contentedly and drew up his legs onto the soft contours of the sofa and numerous cushions.

'Everything looks cosy in here,' said Johann, going over to the fireplace. 'I'll get this lighted.'

Russell looked on as Johann rearranged paper, wood and a few pieces of coal to a satisfactory beginning. The flame flickered immaturely but didn't falter. All Johann's education had taught him to strive in small things.

Russell looked on. They had both released themselves from a muddy, reedy punt hunt in an early evening chill. This scene was a warm-up for something bigger.

'Wonder what's upstairs?' said Russell from the sofa as Johann coaxed the reassuring flames from the previously dead fireplace. 'What a maze this place must be.'

'We'll see it in the light tomorrow,' said Johann, lying back with greater equanimity. He had provided the light.

'It won't take much to stir up this place.' said Russell in a mock mysterious tone. 'Perhaps we can tickle it a bit in the dark?'

'What do you mean?' asked Johann.

'I'll bet you anything you like, there's a something here,' said Russell as he put his arms right back over his shoulders to catch at the arm rest.

Johann got up from the carpet to mirror Russell on the adjacent couch. He stretched his back and legs on the unfamiliar furniture belonging to the parents of a recently made acquaintance. University life was like that from his now lengthy perspective. Friends came and went. The undergraduate years were open, volatile, crazy. Even so, he wasn't altogether ready for Russell's next remark.

'Let's dowse it out. Let's conjure it about.'

'What? Russell? What are you talking about?' said Johann, who couldn't get comfortable. He had felt better squatting by the light of the fire.

'I mean get the house-spirit to join us. Just us.' Russell went on. 'It'd never work with six. Nicola's too dogmatic, Peter's too eager to please and Nat and Daniel are newbies. You know what I mean.'

Johann lurched forward to hunch up on his knees. His now roaring fire was the only known point in the room.

'So, how'd you know what to do?' said Johann. Looking sideways at Russell, he was surprised to see how intent he was.

'You just ask. Relax and ask. I've done it before. They come, then go.'

Russell sounded very sure of himself in this completely new situation. He'd never set foot in this old house before. Where did this assurance come from?

Johann was to regret what he then said.

'Go ahead.' He swung his legs off his sofa to face Russell on his.

Russell looked up at the embossed ceiling. The flames flickered in a quickly darkening dusk. The leaded window of the west wing picked up the dying light of a February day. It was five thirty on the mantelpiece clock.

'Come and find us,' whispered Russell to the air and the clock faintly whirred the half hour.

'It can't be hard to find,' said Johann as lightly as he could. His tone was not a participatory one.

'We're here,' said Russell, seeming not to hear Johann.

Johann got up from the bench by the pond and stepped forward a couple of paces. He saw the green water of the pond turn purple just as he had seen the dull air of the sitting room at Upwell Hall that evening take on a violet hue. It was no colour of the sunset. It was brought from a space which was unknown and Russell had started even more than he did.

'Look, Johann, we've been heard,' came his voice. 'The light has changed.'

Russell slowly eased himself up, got off the sofa to face Johann fully and tried to stand upright. The purple light seemed to press heavily on him and the twenty one year old Economics student felt himself a different height.

'That's one comfy sofa,' said Russell as a hint of fear came into his eyes. 'I can hardly straighten up.'

He walked over to the fire very slowly and sat down on the fender seat. He turned to look at Johann, who was about to join him by the fire.

'No, don't come too close. I'm not right, you can see,' he said firmly to Johann.

About his head was a purple sheen, as if the warmth of the fire was irradiating some latent hair gel or other masculine toiletry. There was no light from the window now. The room was lit by the fire and the unnatural lavender glow of Russell's head of hair.

'What do you think you've done?' said Johann cautiously. This was not Russell's colouring when they had explored these unknown rooms only twenty minutes ago. A subdued young man transfixed in front of a roaring fire did not look like a recipe for an adventurous weekend. If the adventure had already begun, then a conclusion was very necessary.

Hands in his pockets, Johann stood, his backpack on the bench. He resembled the eternal student philosopher, reflecting the myriad of folk long sinced passed on the ancient drovers' road, rooted in landscape and its continual movement, not perplexity.

His dismay with Russell was put to one side as he stood at the fireside.

'What can you see? he said to Russell, whose shoulders sagged perceptibly.

'It's not good, Johann,' came the reply. 'It's a purple pinpoint of light with a halo round it, like you'd see a police car light through a misty window. It won't shift from the centre of my vision. It's funny, Johann, but I can't see it if I stare at the fire.'

'We'll get you out of this fix,' said Johann.

'I got myself into it, like a fool. I can't expect you to help me out,' said Russell. 'I'm a sucker for this sort of thing. Give me a dark room and I think I'm in charge.' His voice was strong, but he was facing the fire.

Johann heard voices and footsteps from the dining room, where a log was being heaved on the fire. Then Nicola came through with her light step.

'Oh, you're in here. It looks great. Come through and we'll get supper.'

Johann moved off in the direction of the weald. He knew the footpaths well. He saw again the fuss of making supper that night. Russell had to move from the fire and was set to peeling potatoes like a scullion, but at least it kept him sat down. All the cooking was done efficiently but not to the detriment of their enthusiasm for discussion away from tutors and tutorials. Russell's lack of engagement wasn't noticed until a citron dessert made its way to the table. Nat bore it from the modern fridge in the parents' quarters which were unseen by paying visitors to the property.

'I'll try some,' replied Russell, but his greying face was noticeable now. 'I'll turn in then. I'll need an early night, I think.'

'Show us where we're sleeping,' said Johann to Nicola. 'I'll be back when I've made sure he's OK.'

'Fine,' said Nicola and strode off lightly enough up a flight of servants' stairs to show them a string of rooms along the very top of the house. She turned on the passage light and then those in the two adjacent rooms.

'See you downstairs later, Johann. The others have got ideas to put to you, especially Nat,' said Nicola as she turned to go. 'Hope you feel better soon, Russell.'

It was quite clear to Johann that Russell couldn't be easily cured of anything in this state and his friend was getting weaker with fear.

Johann was moving upwards now, along a footpath that was about to open onto a full view of the weald. He had loved the surprise all his open air life and, as he looked for the space which opened the vista, he saw Russell's face that night.

'Can you help? If anyone can, it's you,' said Russell as he lay down on the bed in that small room. He closed his eyes and grimaced immediately.

He didn't need to tell Johann what he saw. 'I'm done in. I'll never sleep again if you can't help me.'

The old bed creaked as he moved to get comfortable.

Putting melodrama firmly out of his mind, Johann moved slowly in the room, picking up Russell's carrier bag of clothes and placing it on a chair at the side of the bed.

'Try to rest,' he said. 'I'll get back to the others so they don't guess anything. What I'm going to do is ask Nicola about the house. It's so old, it must have a Chapel or a room that was one once. We're going to need that for this, Russell.'

Russell turned over on the bed in acquiescence. Johann saw his head on the pillow tingeing the cream linen a deep indigo and he turned quickly to leave.

It was towards 2am that the others were ready to go upstairs. Johann had made enquiries during conversations which were lively in the very manner Nicola had intended. Her boyfriend, a studious musician, had enthralled her with his grasp of philosophy from Johann's impromptu tutorials. Concentrating her mind on this, she airily told Johann a bit about the Elizabethan heritage of the building. The old Chapel was a small back room just down from the third set of stairs to the servants' area. Fortunately it wasn't used for storage. Russell's original remark about a maze of rooms was correct and Johann needed to guide Russell through it.

As the prospect opened up, Johann breathed more easily, shifting his backpack and stopping to shuffle his feet exactly where he always did with his family on walks to this point. Russell's world had to come back into view like this one, making a wider angle for the eye upon it.

Upstairs, he tiptoed over to Russell at about 3am. It was a blackness he could deal with, that seeing sense of velvet when objects soften up at nearness. He shook Russell, but knew he was not sleeping at all.

'Got it, Johann?' said Russell urgently.

'Yes. When you get up, hold my jacket at the back. We can't have any light. There are stairs,' he cautioned quietly in reply.

'I'd climb a skyscraper for an end to this,' said Russell in a low voice. He wanted an out-of-doors reality back as quickly as possible.

The older student led the younger to the end of the corridor away from the rooms used by the three other guests. At least Nicola, who knew every creak of the house, was down in her family's wing of the house. Just as Johann's eyes became accustomed to the darkness he was aware of an opening.

'Stairs now, Russell,' he said, nudging Russell so he was quite clear about the next step. The two young men shuffled down each with one arm out to hold the curving bannister. At the bottom they stood to take stock. Johann touched the walls each side hoping to find a light switch and then felt a double one on a forward wall. He switched on both together. Immediately he saw the stairs and corridor.

'Aah,' - Russell stifled his cry.

'Let me help,' said Johann quickly and took his friend by the shoulders facing him. He didn't want Russell to overbalance in the sudden glare.

It was a necessity. Nicola's description wasn't too accurate in regard to steps up and down. Once Russell was steady on his feet, Johann left him to briefly check the four doors he could see on either side. Two were cupboards. One room had wooden chairs around a large leather topped desk and the fourth had just what he wanted, emptiness.

Johann quickly got Russell to come, walking slowly beside him for a few steps, then he leaned quickly backwards so as to turn off the two switches. With blackness so immediate, he didn't want to move upwards as quickly but came round to Russell's right arm like a companionable canine friend, asking nothing but to be there. Any untoward pressure now would lead to an error. Johann led Russell into the empty room and all that was required was to sense it and then see it dimly as a room with proportion and meaning.

The two of them could not sit down. There were no sofas as had earlier brought this about, but a space, contained and secure. It should be enough, Johann sensed, but Russell had to know it too.

Russell moved in a little further. Johann felt the bulk of his body placed forward of him, but didn't follow. Trained in initiative in just this way at school, he found himself responding to Russell's minute endeavours to be rid of the puzzling light. In this room, doubtless blessed with prayer and individual means of striving over centuries, only a truth as clear as the light was needed to free him. There were twenty minutes of blackening silence before there was a sneeze. Johann promptly sensed Russell's arm raised to cuff at his nose and then the turn of the body to him.

'Gone,' said Russell.

Johann, standing before the view to conclude the story of the old Hall, smiled slightly just as he did at Russell in the early hours of that morning. He set off up the slopes, a man of coming and going just like those who had made the paths he knew so well. Many of them knew that a wise man wonders at the wise.

Back home for supper, Anton was teasing his mother.

'We said you'd gone for good this time, Johann, and that you wouldn't be back. The dissertation would be left for your tutor to finish and how would we feel about that?' Anton chopped celery in the kitchen with a deliberate downward cut onto a wooden board.

'I told Anton not to worry so much when you're out for only a day, especially this lovely weather,' said Shirley as she got ready to toss a salad. 'Anton missed you. When do you have to go back?'

'It'll be Saturday.' said Johann. 'There's plenty to do and I have to go back up to London for the British Library twice a week.'

Anton saw him off that day. The rail journey to London was commuter heaven. It was easy to get a fast train, but a local stopping one gave Johann time to reflect.

Nicola met him in the town again a few weeks later, at the beginning of April.

'Can you come up for the weekend of the 30th?' she asked him. 'I've got the others on the hook. Can we entice you?'

Johann was more than ready to go. If the house could accommodate those friends and their natural youthful tendency to set the thinkers right, then he was comfortable. Russell would perhaps be wary, but the year was marching beyond Spring into a different light.

That Friday in April, Johann sat on the mid-morning train to London, just catching his breath. The day was fair. The countryside soon passed into Berkshire's rounded woods and dells with their shade and room for bluebells.

Johann's train was less than a quarter full at this time of day. It stopped at almost all stations to Reading, then on to London non-stop. Johann was reading a book when the train jarred and he looked up at a blinding light. It drew him to the window and then he went right through it. It took his life with mercilessly spearing thick glass when his train left the rails just before the station. Of the seven killed and many injured, his was the body found on the tracks.

In the evening of the same day, Nicola, Peter and Russell stood by Upwell Hall moat. Nat and Daniel were walking towards them over the short bridge. They all sat down at the water's edge, upright at first, watching the light of evening repeating in the water, then lying on their backs to look at the cloud-filled sky. Nothing was said.

'He knew about the light,' said Russell clearly and turned to lay his face down on the slope, his fists clenched to white upon the grass.

# Rowing Blue

It wasn't Deborah's way to be critical. She liked to give praise, encourage, cajole. Blatant criticism doesn't suit a teacher of piano.

'I think I'll just have to give this one up, Jack.' She spoke rather curtly to her husband at supper. 'I can't get him to play a single thing right. I don't just mean the notes, He doesn't seem to understand the piano. How he got to Grade Five with his previous teacher, I don't know.'

She got up to feed the cat who'd come in by the flap.

'Some just learn by rote, don't they, then it catches up with them.' said John.

He'd had this conversation before. The cat flap had opened before. He looked at Deborah bent over her task and said, 'I'm off out. Don's got us all to sing ready for Easter.'

'All right, John,' said Deborah uneasily, without turning. 'I'll see you later.'

As she fed the cat, Deborah debated John's movements. When their two sons had been growing up he'd been as predictable as feeding the cat. There were nightly suppers, musical evenings and all the play of a family life with expectations, especially her mother's.

'Practice time, Alex,' she'd call or John would call. Now the tune was as discordant as the pianos at her pupils' houses.

'Your mother says it's time for practice. Are you going to get down here or not?' John called now, distancing himself so very subtly from his wife of twenty years.

'Here's a hitch and an itch.' The nagging thought kept occurring to her. 'We'd always worked it together until about a year ago.'

Could Deborah date it? Probably not accurately at all. The grating phrase, the quick swipe of a book off the piano. Heedless discord taken at face value and in your face. 'Eastenders' unfortunately came to mind.

'It's in your face, Debbie. 'E's not lookin' at you anymore!'

The cat slipped upstairs. Deborah went to her piano and sat at the desk alongside. The letter which had arrived only yesterday smiled up from its headed notepaper.

'Winfield House, Worcester'.

She liked the sound of that. The letter, too, was completely agreeable. The five bedroom home was to be let to them at a reasonable price for the duration of the Festival Week they'd chosen. Six of her friends, instrumentalists, liked the idea of a week playing quartets for their enjoyment in the spaces between the Festival concerts. It all felt right. It just had to go right.

Deborah wrote the cheque to a Mr. Sebastian Johnson and then the quick postcards to her contacts. There was a young married couple, a divorcee, Judith, returned from the U.S, two Sixth formers at the same Co-Ed School and herself. It was planned for the School Summer holidays. John would be elsewhere. She'd let him know about the car.

Summer holidays don't figure largely in a Music teacher's life. The money may or may not be available and the chance of extra tuition cannot be ignored. John hadn't planned the usual camping in France even last year, so the boys had found a camping holiday with friends and were following it up this year, too, excitedly communicating their plans. Deborah felt that the wellyboot was on the wrong foot as she planned her solo holiday, ironically a joint visit to a Musical Week in a famously musical town.

Deborah squeezed the polite teenagers, Katie and Robert, into her car. Judith had picked up the young couple in hers and a convoy performance followed, cross country from Olney to Worcester, stopping at a pub for an early lunch. Deborah began to relax. English food, then English music and international conductors. She smiled at her thoughts while chatting to teenagers about the limits of pub cuisine.

She backed into the driveway of Winfield House. Red brick, just like her own house, but of different proportions; she felt as if she had come to a home and had come home. A brighter light seemed to push the house forward into her crowded thoughts, emptying them for itself. All the chat of unloading; the 'This is mine,' passed her by. She needed nothing but what this house was. No longer the assurance of a cheque, a piece of paper in the post, but an area of earth piled high with brick and holding a treasure or two for her.

'Looks good, doesn't it.' stated Robert, trying to set the scene and thinking about his 'phone call home to Mum.

'It'll hold us all, that's for sure,' replied Deborah, trying to be herself as her thoughts seemed not her own.

They trooped inside, finding the solidly square Edwardian house left as if it was the 'Marie Celeste.' The family had gone on holiday, but evidently trusted their guardians to observe house rules. Very little had been moved to accomodate strangers.

Robert and Katie got themselves a drink and went into the garden. The others went to their rooms upstairs, leaving Deborah with the ground floor to herself.

The others hadn't even looked around, home makers though some of them must be. Deborah was meant to scrutinise, to make it all her own. She ignored her bags in the hall, even her black bulging handbag safely removed from its special place in the car. She began in the first room. The threshold throbbed and a catch in her throat forced her to take a breath.. Over the mantelpiece was fixed a very large oar with light blue stripes on the handle. Sebastian was a Rowing Blue, she realised, and the man became a presence to her, a moving, heaving bulk. His boat rowed towards her in the film set of her mind, just steered by the cox to pass her by and negotiate the door.

She shook her head in surprise.

'It's wonderful to watch a family growing up like this,' she murmured while deliberately going from photo to photo, from frame to frame, to evaluate a family life not her own. She tossed her head to shake off the blatantly adolescent wows of surprise and inexperience as her mouth opened to say more. It came to her that she engaged with a family whose shadowy simplicity, progression and march through the differing years of graduation, marriage, child rearing and certificates of prowess was shown by a mixture of photos which she made orderly for herself.

'Oh, yes,' to each. To the name of the Cambridge College, the architecture of the Church porch, the colour of the school uniform, the myriad of faces of Matriculation and sports team photos and all tastefully interspersed with a paraphernalia of ornaments, jotters and good looking pens and pencils.

She retreated to the doorway to take another overview, trying to be herself instead of the wife of a Cambridge Blue.

'This'll be our playing room.' The phrase appeared to come, not from the weakly under-engaged woman who had just driven two teenagers to this house, but from a strongly-rooted musician, a woman who knew her place at the piano and at the family table. All the fidget in her had gone in embracing that room. She could not only live with this, she could love herself with it. Coveting perfection as all pianists do, Deborah had found it without even striking a note. The room had a chord all of its own.

Deborah went round to the piano, a good upright placed behind the opening door so that light from the bay window easily reached the propped music.

'We'll have duos and trios here. That'll be easy,' she thought, then snapped back to her handbag, unpacking, where was the programme of the first concert and where were the tickets for that evening's recital?

The group met in an airy sitting room to decide on jobs and chores. The teenagers certainly looked happy at taking up this invitation during School holidays. They could have been in Timbuctu for all its strangeness, but also they deemed it as cosy as in their own home. Its comfortable occupation as a home was imprinted on every room. The only danger would be leaving their own possessions around in the companionable scrum and then have to hunt interminably for them so as to leave at the end of the week.

Deborah considered what is put down around you, staking a personal space amid the dance of atoms. Her sheet music scores, sonatas and songs were a lifetime's collection. Each of her sons had played this jig or that minuet at an age she could confidently pinpoint. Where was John on the page?

Deborah took up the shopping reins on that first day. The couple went to explore the distance to the Cathedral with the teenagers and Judith set to on cooking preparation and table laying. It was best to start up an industrious mode.

At the local shops Deborah shopped for the Johnson's family of five. In the Delicatessen she chose vegetarian items and unusual antipasti as if their tastes were Mediterranean and healthy. The two cheeses she offered them were strong, not bland, and the bread rolls as rustic as from the baker's oven from that very morning; as far from John's white sliced as a millstone by the pond. She did make tracks to the butchers, though, thinking Sebastian would appreciate a few lamb chops in batter as an end of week treat. By then it would be a finale for them, so it was imperative to have a wine.

At the greengrocers a local produce counter prompted her to look at jams and chutneys with gingham hoods, gaily challenging a guess at their contents.

'Quince,' she said to the assistant. 'I know it's good with cheese.'

'Yes, it really is,' she replied.

Deborah knew her as a friend it seemed.

Worcester's farming district brought a wonder of choice in this local shop and Deborah enjoyed its end of July harvest.

'Hasn't the weather been good for soft fruits?' she said to another assistant who was weighing out.

'Certainly good round here,' she said, then, 'Are you making a pie?'

'I may very well,' replied Deborah, surprised at herself.

Back at Winfield House she unloaded for Judith and, for once, had a discussion which wasn't about music.

'What a place we've chosen,' said Deborah with a smile.

'You mean it's big enough for us all?' Judith was packing into the fridge. 'It's a pity John couldn't come.'

Deborah looked at the head of her musical acquaintance, edgily enough to read a great deal into the remark.

'He always plans to be somewhere else,' said Deborah before Judith turned to see her face.

Deborah looked again at the solidity of this kitchen. It was not particularly modernised, but it had the fresh look of constant use and centrality. She sat down at the pine table with the fruit bowl and its bananas.

'Pity the Worcester apples aren't ready yet.' Deborah was making the locality hers and Judith sensed the reason for it. Seasons hadn't fallen into place often for her and seasons admit that reassurance year on year.

'I suppose you think this is the perfect home,' began Judith, at once eager to take on the challenge of conversation as well as wash the salad for the evening.

Deborah decided to open the door a chink. She went over to it.

'It's not so much that. It's just that it seems like a working home which makes other things work. We all have squabbles.'

Judith was beginning to chop runner beans.

'When Josh went off, I felt I couldn't make another home ever. A house for one simply isn't homely,' she said, and reached for the salad onions.

Deborah felt she had to say more to this woman she'd only known for a very short time, there being a once weekly attendance at her Music Group.

'Some homes are for one when all the beds are full.'

Then Deborah left the table.

'I hope I got you enough for an early supper. We'll be in time for tonight's concert at 7pm in the Cathedral.' She said genially as she left the room.

In the front room a little later, Deborah set up the ring of music stands around the piano for the coming hour. Early afternoon sunlight showed the room at its best. It was usable for almost every endeavour; a tea time, a sherry party, a family chinwag, a Great Aunt's retreat. As a Music room it had so many listeners in the photographs. Their self-interest in their own lives meant that performances would need to be bold and accurate to afford them a smile. Deborah smiled rather as they did and went upstairs to change.

On the final evening, the two teenagers were to give a rendition, Robert on piano and Katie on violin. It would be a programme of their choosing. Deborah set up the room after Robert's brief practising. Katie was bowing away upstairs. It had been a really successful week. The Johnsons did seem to smile at the impromptu concert for them.

After the Three Choirs' final afternoon the small company could all relax and settle themselves for their journey home.

Deborah looked around with the same eyes as on that first day, but was a new, self-demanding Deborah of life in this family home. The dominating oar caught her attention as before. She looked at its blue stripes, the curve of the paddle and its sheer length and strength. She wouldn't be able to see it again. In the three year cycle of the Festival's return to Worcester, she'd be a very different person, and the family photos might add another wedding, perhaps even a grandchild over that time.

Her future stalled, almost like a boat without a paddle. She thought of the meadow and river at Olney, then her thoughts took her over the fields to nearby Bedford where the river broadened for the use of scullers and river rowers before widening towards Ely and the Wash. That was the rower's way, the way back home, following the practising Cambridge Blues. She needed muscle for her particular oar, to take up a different way of life without John now and to row away, dipping firmly into choppy water. She'd have to accept the cold breeze until she came to the finish line, an individual winner.

# London Buses

'Ger 'er on then,' came the voice of the 'bus conductor and Bennie looked up at him as he stood aside on the platform to let the little girl step up the big step onto the 'bus, helped by her mother.

'Liverpool Street?' asked the mother briefly.

Bennie stepped up behind the young mother, waited until they had both sat down in their choice of seat and then sat alongside them.

'Good morning, Dr. Walstein,' said the young mother politely to Bennie, as he knew she would.

'Mrs. Wilson, isn't it, and Patsy?' Bennie wanted it correct.

'Yes, I brought 'er in for the 'hooping a couple of months ago. Now we're getting about more, 'cos it's warmer,' replied the mother.

'That should do the trick,' said Bennie and looked at Patsy.

'Where are you off to, Doctor? Is it a patient?' said Mrs. Wilson.

'I'm catching a train. This 'bus gets me there in good time,' said Bennie.

'Now there's a place to make 'er cough. All them fumes,' smiled Mrs. Wilson as she adjusted herself to get off for the next stop.

As she rose and got hold of Patsy, Bennie got up, too, to acknowledge a lady leaving. Mrs. Wilson nodded to him.

'Can't say 'See you soon',' she smiled politely, getting Patsy just between her knees to steady her. 'Regards to your wife.'

It was Shoreditch Road, her stop.

Bennie went on to Liverpool Street Station for a journey to Golders Green by Tube. He always found it claustrophobic but today the escalator stairs were a little more daunting as he tipped slightly when he raised his right foot to step on it. Bennie held the rail on the right as fast moving persons went down on the left. He was aiming to visit an uncle who kept up contact despite Bennie's unusual position in the family circle. Uncle Sim was proud of Bennie and didn't hide it. Now in his eighties, he liked to be visited just before Shabbat once a month. The Tube train got Bennie there with no trouble, as long as he didn't trip again.

Sim's house was a pleasant one. The housekeeper let him in. As he stepped up, leaving the suburban street for a lighted hallway, he consciously raised his right foot a little higher, even though he had crossed this threshold many times before.

'Good afternoon, Ethel,' he said as his foot came down onto the scrubbed hall floor.

'Good afternoon, Dr. Walstein,' nodded Ethel and she led Bennie into the drawing room.

'Ah, Bennie. So good. You're here now,' said the figure just about to rise from a fireside chair. 'Thank you, Ethel.'

Sim looked hard at his sister's boy as he got himself upright.

'You've reached fifty, you devil.'

'Yes, that's right,' replied Bennie, motioning his uncle to sit and sitting down himself in a facing easy chair. 'I'll soon be needing more rest in one of these.' He smiled at Sim. 'How are you?'

'With your sharp eyes, you can see well enough, Bennie. I'm coughing a bit more than I'd like, but I'll live,' said Sim, settling back in his chair.

Sim's bald head was caught in the light of a side lamp as he leaned back. His suit reveres of a wartime cut moved up with the shoulder pads as he shifted in the chair.

'And your stress levels, Bennie?' said Sim as he looked at his nephew sitting forward in his chair. 'You were a bit shaky when you came last time. I hope that's all cleared up. How's Margaret?'

'She's fine. I'm fine,' replied Bennie, whose thin frame scarcely fitted the capacious chair. He pulled up his trousers from above the knee with a deft pinch of his fingers. Margaret had picked out black socks that morning for his trip. She was a loyal wife who understood the reason for the monthly Shabbat visit.

'How's the Synagogue doing?' Bennie's query gave Sim lots of scope.

'All's going well and no small thanks to you, Bennie. That was a good heft last year,' said Sim and pointed to a sherry decanter on the table beside him. 'Any?'

'No, thank you,' said Bennie. 'I'm happy to give from as far away as Dalston. We're opening the Surgery another half day and Margaret's helping me with the cover, but I'm finding the trek a long one. I've thought all the thoughts, Sim, and I've done all that's expected by the family. I may have to cut down.' Bennie wished he did have a glass of sherry to wash down that confession and he sat back to compensate.

'You've done more than enough, Bennie. God save Myra's soul, she'd have been so proud,' said Sim as he made to get up.

Bennie came forward quickly from the depths of his armchair, so that Sim didn't see his shaking hand reach for its wooden arm. He was up and taking Sim's elbow before Sim's head was raised.

'Time to go over,' said Sim.

After the Synagogue visit, the reading and a brief look at some new investment in an outbuilding, Bennie left Sim to return to the Tube Station. He called in, as usual, to the local Bakery.

'Seeded pretzels? I'll have six,' he said to the assistant, whom he knew well.

'Put in an order for next time,' said Ruthie with a smile of encouragement as Bennie paid.

Later, at Liverpool Street Station, there was a wait for the Dalston 'bus in the road outside. Some 'buses hadn't turned around, but had gone on up to the City. Bennie held his briefcase down, looking up and beyond the boundary Church to spot the red behind the blackness of the queuing taxis at the far crossing lights. London streets were his streets, a pendulum of traffic seen once and over again in a rhythm which had dominated his life there.

He had met and married Margaret when she'd come over from Canada ten years after the War, a war which took both his parents. It was a marriage for business and companionship. There were so many babies then and a need for the local GP Surgeries to enlarge, especially in

London. Bennie had aquired a substantial corner building which had escaped the bombing of several surrounding streets. The new flats held the young patients. Margaret's steely Presbyterian upbringing gave her a stoic work ethic and the pair made a sound beginning just as they were entering their forties, partnering as Doctors and man and wife. 'Walstein and Walstein' clearly had to be termed rather softer with Margaret's maiden name of Yorke, and so it was that Bennie hailed the 'bus to return him to 'Drs. Yorke and Walstein', De Beauvoir Road, Dalston E8, one of the busiest practices in the area.

'Margaret, how's the afternoon Surgery been?' he said immediately as he came in and saw her in the far kitchen down the hall.

'Take off your coat first, Bennie,' said Margaret, walking up quickly towards him to give him a peck on the cheek. 'Of course it's been all right,' she said as she helped him off with his mackintosh. 'It just overran by about half an hour, but Mrs. Cowley came by with some laundry as it happened and she made me a mug of coffee, bless her.'

'Good,' said Bennie. 'Your staple.'

'Sit down for a bit after the 'bus journey, Bennie. I've got everything on. Mrs. Cowley even peeled the potatoes. It's fish pie,' said his wife.

'Christian Friday,' smiled Bennie to Margaret.

'Not exactly, you old soul. It's just bits and pieces from the market on Tuesday,' she replied and poured her husband a glass of sherry when he nodded.

'Put it down on the table, Margaret. I'll pick it up in a moment or two,' said Bennie.

They sat over supper with a glass of white wine each. The glasses were from Westphalia. How they had survived so long was a family joke before the death of his parents.

'It's the most fragile which lasts,' his mother used to muse when she picked up the thin stems and twisted the crystal bowls.

'You cannot compare, Mamma,' he once replied. 'You've had nothing else fragile which has broken. What happens out of sight is out of mind.'

'You're a literalist, Benjamin,' she'd said. 'You always were.'

Somewhere in Germany, shattered into many pieces, were the red wine, the goblets and liqueur glasses of the complete set, and their six white wine glasses remained. Margaret kept them safely in a cabinet with the silver from her family, heirlooms easily traceable to Scots who had pitched up in Canada to do just what they did at home. It hadn't been quite that easy for the Walsteins.

'Tomorrow, after Surgery, we'll have a lunch, Bennie,' said Margaret. 'I've invited the Youth Group for a Bonfire Party in our garden. I did tell you a few weeks ago,' said Margaret.

'Yes, I remember,' said Bennie. 'Here's to them. You do them proud.' His hand trembled slightly as he raised his glass. Margaret had turned from the table to pick up a leaflet. She shook it open.

'Yes, it is this weekend. They want to help clear the garden, light a bonfire and cook up some baked potatoes. They'll use the kitchen, Bennie, if you're about.'

'Oh, I'll be round about,' said Bennie.

He didn't at all resent Margaret's philanthropic efforts. She contributed to the teenagers at her Church. Some hadn't seen a garden in London, or not a big area like theirs. It lay at the rear and side of their corner plot, producing far too much buddleia and ivy in its time of neglect. Long-legged youth wouldn't take too long to flatten it if not to cut it back. He wasn't expecting finesse.

'I'll see what tools are in the shed,' Bennie remarked as he left the table and shuffled the chair beneath it.

The next morning, surgery was on overrun by more than an hour. Mrs. Cowley's planned cold chicken was to hand.

'Perfect,' said Margaret as she delivered it to the table. 'Take what you want, Bennie and I'll have some, too. Will you carve?'

' No, you do it, Margaret. You'll know how much,' said Bennie.

Later that afternoon, just as it was greying into early Autumn evening, Margaret drove up with four of the group. The teenagers came up to the side gate. They stood waiting awkwardly as Dr. Yorke put her car in the garage at the bottom of the garden. Looking out of the Surgery Waiting

Room bay window, Bennie saw the boys, hands in pockets, staring up the road. He went out the front door to meet them by going down the two steps.

'It's up here. She won't be long, but the garage door is stiff.' He indicated the few steps up. He intended to lead the way back up, but something stopped him. His right leg stayed at three inches above the ground and wouldn't go further. He placed the foot back down on the path.

'Go on in,' he said, waving this time to the door and hall. 'Go straight through to the kitchen at the end. Get yourself a pot of tea.'

'Thanks, sir,' the boys said as the girls went ahead smiling. They guessed this man was Dr. Walstein. He knew they wouldn't want a formal introduction. Margaret would ease it over, thought Bennie as he turned off to the Surgery to get on with letters.

Later that evening the bonfire was a success it seemed. Bennie watched from an upstairs window as the flames showed up their garden as good as it had been for some time, empty of debris for an approaching winter. He turned from the window a little stiffly, then found his right foot unable to move forward. It stayed poised as if waiting for a foot mark to appear or, like one of Sim's angels, Bennie very fleetingly reflected, awaiting the wing's folding presence behind before alighting beside the tent. Sim was good on angels.

'They're just going,' the call came up from Margaret at the bottom of the stairs.

She had planned a short walk for the bunch of ten to get to the 'bus stop in the dark. She could not offer to drive them all back. Bennie had been asked earlier in the day to accompany them to the 'bus stop in Kingsland Road so as to see her back home.

Bennie began to walk down the stairs. The brown carpet felt firm under his feet until he oddly misplaced his right foot on the bottom step.

'Damn,' said Bennie as he felt his ankle twist slightly.

'Are you all right, dear?' came Margaret's voice.

Bennie replied with a loud grunt.

The members of the Youth Group jostled along the road with the doctors chaperoning, shepherding, following on behind. It felt like a leading onward; job done, fire laid, fire burned, fire out, food consumed and the children go forward. Bennie's own footsteps echoed his patter of thought.

'Goodbye. I'll be there on Sunday,' called Margaret to them as the teenagers slid into the upstairs seats to wave down at them from the steamed windows.

'That's good,' observed Bennie as he turned with Margaret.

'I'm pleased,' replied his wife.

Friday afternoon that week, Bennie set off on another 'bus journey. It was to take him to the West End. It involved a couple of changes from Dalston Junction to which he had walked after lunch. He missed a few 'buses that day.

'Can you get on it, please, mate?' said the first of the conductors.

Bennie stood close to the platform of the 'bus, both feet on the pavement, unable to persuade either foot to raise itself high enough to reach the wood and plastic of the wide ledge. He let go of the centre pole.

The conductor rang the bell impatiently. 'Make up your mind next time!' he called as the 'bus moved off.

Bennie waited for the next.

Margaret had the car that afternoon for home visits. Bennie was not altogether expecting to be so out of sorts. He did better with the second 'bus and settled in a corner, thinking of Sim and his fireside chair, the sherry glass and the simple routine of hospitality.

When Bennie arrived at Dr. Nyman's Practice in Harley Street, a white-uniformed nurse greeted him.

'Come in, Dr. Walstein. You're early. Please sit here. Dr. Nyman won't keep you waiting beyond your appointment time.'

Bennie looked round at the fixtures and fittings, the very bright strip lighting above and the glass table top at knee height in front of him. Reassuringly bright, an October sun streamed in at the window. The room was full of uploading light. It re-defined the waiting area oppressed with glare, almost the same as if it were thoughtful gloom.

'It's good to see you again, Len,' said Bennie to his old friend and former colleague.

'East End still East, is it?' smiled Len as he sat down behind his desk. He watched Bennie jerk himself down on the chair provided.

'Yes, but it's still denying 'West is Best',' replied Bennie. He paused. 'East or West, what's the long and the short of it, Len?' Bennie leaned forward onto his friend's desk.

'Tests show positive, Bennie. I can't make them do otherwise,' Len replied and pushed Bennie's Medical folder across the table to him. His smile had faded. 'There are ways through this. Exercise and medication can make one hell of a difference.'

'I can't do my job, though, Len. It's something my patients would spot a mile off. How long do you think before I'll be forced to give up? I need time to train a replacement in the Practice.' Bennie pushed back the folder as he spoke, not expecting an answer to his question.

'No-one could say,' Len said. 'Predictions have been proved unreliable and research is badly funded. You know all this.'

Bennie sat farther back in his chair and Len did the same. The two men looked at each other with the warmth of memory and relaxed.

'None of this is good news,' said the Harley Street Doctor.

'Even expected news is news. Confirmation being justification,' replied the GP from Dalston and they each stood up in their respective roles.

Bennie held on to the desk as he stood.

'Well, thank you, Len. That'll do for now.'

'Come any time,' said Len as he moved to open the door. 'My regards to Margaret.'

It was just the two 'buses back to Dalston Junction, but it was getting busier as shoppers headed home, eyeing the dark.

'Take yer time. Take yer time,' The first 'bus conductor strove to count on his speeding customers and moved an arm to fend off more than he needed.

'I'll let you on then, mate,' he said to Bennie, who stood uncertainly. 'I'll give you an 'and up 'ere.'

Bennie had to stand with the four in the five person line just inside the entrance to the 'bus. He held onto the strap and swayed as he'd always done, feet set apart to balance and not crash into anyone's lap.

Back home, Margaret came to the door encouragingly when she heard him come in.

'You're later than I thought you'd be. It's crowded. Everything's speeding up out there, just as it always does at this time of year.'

Bennie next met more of the Youth Group at a New Year Party. It was held at De Beauvoir Road. Margaret had opened the doors between lounge and dining room and had cleared the sofas of Bennie's books. The young took over with the music, the tray food, the laughter and the dancing.

This time Margaret was there for a full introduction to all.

'I think most of you know my husband, Dr. Walstein,' she said brightly and let him wander over to the window seat to edge out of the way.

Bennie watched them engage with the furniture, awkwardly sitting sidesaddle on dining chairs or caressing chairbacks with hands that were needed to steady the legs perching on the chair arm.

Their jerkiness was entertaining and eloquent. Youngsters very slightly out of their depth match each other very well. They sense the camaraderie needed for a strange place, like passengers in a broken down 'bus might anticipate an unfamiliar route to get them home.

Bennie made his excuses and went upstairs. The parents had arranged joint travel back later and were pleased to have had a party arranged by the Walsteins. It would take its course in his home.

The monthly trip to Uncle Sim was in the second week of January, but this time Bennie did not alight at Golders Green Station. He stayed on the train until the end of the line to Edgware. Next to Edgware Station is a large Bus Station built in the 1930s and enlarged in following years.

Anyone who travels regularly on London 'buses knows about the bustle of changing drivers, the early mornings when each 'bus shoots off in a hurry and the ambling nightly habit when 'buses come home like owls go, individual, lonely, silently. The 'buses pull in as if they have been to Timbuktu and back just to deposit one unlucky stranger upon Depot soil.

Bennie came to die and to die well. He came round the side of the high raised open-fronted building as soon as he heard a 'bus starting up. It would be reversing out. He made sure that he spotted a conductor on his way to jump up on the platform. Bennie's thin, slight, upright figure in a brown mackintosh quickly lay down in the path of the reversing 'bus, with chest heaved up ready for the rolling wheel. Bennie was crushed by the empty 'bus.

''E done it deliberate, mate,' the conductor said to the shocked driver, when the two of them found him dead and called the ambulance to their Depot.

'I can't tell you how sorry I am,' said Len over the 'phone to Margaret next day. 'There isn't any hope at present for Parkinson's sufferers and his knowledge of his condition must have doubly crippled him, if you understand me. He loved you and his job too well. His body ran out of time to give and he wouldn't have wanted to take.'

'I know,' said Margaret.

# Sugar Tongs

Resembling small crouching dachsunds, Cynthia's collection of silver sugar tongs was arranged on an oval coffee table in her sitting room. Creams, browns and greens in the curtain fabric were muted at their curvaceous shine and further shimmer in the table polish. Their miniature scale took away none of their intimate beauty; touched on an opulent surface, balanced to perfection on each bow and spoon tip. Each one was a masterpiece of delicacy, originality and workmanship to be brought into contact with an unseen lump of sugar. One pair had delicate silver hands instead of spoons with sculpted gloves and a bracelet clearly embossed on the right. Beneath the other glove doubtless lurked a small, shaped watch which ticked away the time it twinkled on the table day by day.

The guardian of these special pieces was Cynthia Lowndes, wife of five years to Henry, whose adored first wife had died a decade earlier. Silver had brought Cynthia and Henry together. They had met in the Silver Vaults of Chancery Lane, deep down where questions are asked and where it's best to validate your buying capacity.

Cynthia was dressed in a longer than fashionable cream wool suit that day. A chiffon scarf with gold threads caught the exact colour of her hair, fashionably dyed but so much her colour and so full and framing to her large-boned face that Henry felt he had to look more than once. So the conversation started.

'I'm here to sell a couple of tea boxes, but I'd rather ask you out to coffee,' said Henry right at the outset. The reflecting surroundings must have given him a gleam in the eye.

'Well, I happen to be selling coffee spoons,' said Cynthia and smiled wryly, 'but I'm also here to add to my collection of sugar tongs. You'd have to be sweet enough.'

It all made sense and the five years rolled by.

Henry sat back in the corner leather seat of his favourite restaurant where he generally went for coffee at 10am.

'It wasn't a bad opener, was it?' he said and looked carefully at a customer of his shop whose coffee stops often coincided with his at the Cupola House. They began a conversation on arrival.

'No, it wasn't at all. I met my wife in London, too,' said the acquaintance, looking towards her.

Henry sat still at the table provided by the restaurant to make a corner seat more companionable. He only moved his arm to reach for the cafetière, then he put the hand safely aside to gaze around.

It was best to arrive at 10am. After that customers from the local villages came in for their lunches on the twice-weekly market days.

'It's a nice morning.'

Henry's statement meant so much about comfort and dependability, thought his companion, who faced him from that next table.

'I'm glad to have got up, in fact, and walked over in good weather.' Henry went on.

It was just the same for the young family. Their boy and girl liked a jaunt in the push-chair.

Their father leaned forward to Henry again.

'You really seem to like this place,' he said with an engaging smile. As a teacher he knew all the opening lines to encourage and develop a young mind. It might work just as well with elderly Henry who sat as a captive audience.

'Well young man,' said Henry, now raising a coffee cup, 'it's been here longer than I have and well before my father got his furnishing business in the town.'

Henry seemed to sink backwards into the polished oak panelled walls of this wide room, which was at the back of the historic town centre house.

Two hundred years before, the Delft tiles would have gleamed in the warmth of a log fire in the recessed fireplace and he might have been plied with more coffee from a basement kitchen. A well-turned, beautifully crafted Seventeenth Century oak staircase went up to the roof space and to the unique cupola level. An eye over the small market town for three centuries, it was no museum but a working restaurant for the working man.

His listener knew that Henry had a small shop nearby, which was where they had first met. Henry wasn't retired exactly, but his more youthful second wife stood behind the counter for him.

'My wife has met yours in the shop,' spoke up the young man. 'It's furnishing material, isn't it?. She's just so fond of fabric.' He nodded towards his wife almost apologetically.

'Mrs. Lowndes chooses well. She's got the London eye for colour. It's taken her a while to settle in this county town. She didn't know my father, couldn't have, you see, but it's an established furniture removals and furnishing firm from before the First War - H. R. Lowndes. Sounds dependable, don't you think?'

His acquaintance was unused to talking to retired business men. His children were beginning to look fidgety by now.

'I didn't realise you did furniture. Your fabric shop is quite small isn't it?'

Henry nodded in reply.

'Oh, yes, but we've got the big house up the road with warehousing tacked on. Is there anything you could do with?'

'We were looking for a bookcase, since you ask,' came the answer.

'Come on up then, Friday evening. Knock at 117 Outgate. We'll be there.'


The house in Outgate rose up red brick and imposing from the wide pavement. Down the side lane where a small bungalow oddly nestled among bushes opposite, the cavernous house with its tall walls dwarfed the one way tarmac of the narrow lane for almost thirty yards.

It was a bright Autumn evening and sunlight twinkled in the top windows. Mr. Lowndes led the couple in to round off all the coincidental coffee conversations by clinching a deal in polished mahogany.

The family looked amazed at what they saw. The two children sensed the dark of the vast rooms at the back of the meandering house and asked to be carried.

'This is a huge place. You'd never believe it.' The husband jogged his six year-old daughter on his shoulder.

'My father got this for a song just after the First War. 1825 it is. We've kept the best furniture. It's stuff left behind from storage, quick sales and house clearance. Bookcases are in here.' said Henry as he opened a broad door.

Empty bookcases rose up in a Dickensian room, smelling of beeswax and dust and proving a supply of mirrors to the children. Mother held her four year old son up to the glazed half dozen or so bookcases ranged round the room.

'Which one shall we have?' she cheerfully spoke to him to put him at his ease. He and they had never seen so comically bizarre a room. It didn't seem to have a function, compounding emptiness with nothingness in its vacant shelving and reluctant polished wood.

Henry helped the family decide on one of the tallest with full drawers below and four shelves in the glazed top. Large brass handles attracted the young boy who got stood down to rattle them.

'I'll be able to get that delivered next week,' said Henry Lowndes as he turned to lead them all back through this imposing house to the street.

As a thank you to their customer, a morning invitation was accepted by the young mother and the two children one day in the week following.

The tongs were placed in ziz-zags across the shiny table. One of their spoon backs resembled two identical fingernails neatly manicured. Cuticles were pressed into silver smoothed roundness. There were no rough edges, no washerwomen's hands here. Instead the finger grips were darted with engraved flowerheads, pointing the way to perfection.

On another pair scallop shells shaped with secure precision to hold the sugar firmly were mirrored beautifully in the table as if it was a rock-pool of clearest water. These would clamp on sugar lumps as firmly as sand particles settle into an oyster shell.

Faint rib marks inside the arms were a feature of another plainly shaped spoon bow, clear of embossing. The interior patterning caressed the slender sides. Perhaps gossamer gloves had held this ephemeral piece for the sugar to dissolve in palest tea.

An acorn head and its twin decorated another pair. The tongs balanced on an embossed silver bow running along with autumn leaves. Robert Adam would have rejoiced at his miniature patterning reflected in this modern unadorned table, an unwitting preserver of real beauty and the best of etiquette.

The two children were sitting quietly and their mother spoke.

'They'll be fine, Mrs. Lowndes. What a wonderful collection. Thank you for inviting us to coffee today.'

'I've just kept this dozen, like Apostles spoons, you might say, but it's two dozen really,' said Mrs. Lowndes.

Her own reflection crossed the shining table as she poured from a tall, slender china pot.

'Henry says you liked the look of our bookcases?' She handed the cup across.

'Yes, thank you,' the young mother replied absentmindedly, placing her coffee cup out of reach.

'We moved to this small bungalow in the side street next to our business when Henry had it built for me. The whole house was far too big for us, but it holds everything left over from the old firm. Henry has run it all down now and we just do the furnishings.'

Mrs. Lowndes wasn't sure why she confided in this mother of two. As a curious visitor to the fabric shop she'd shown an eye for detail, unlike most customers. Memorably, she'd bought twelve yards of a fine red satin with large golden deer running and jumping on it. The way she'd described the twin bed hangings and covers she was going to make made

Mrs Lowndes feel that she was back in London again discussing bold colours and designs. Her usual customers here were not adventurous.

They talked about the children and gave them biscuits.

'Of course, Henry married me five years ago. Five years after his first wife died. I quite like a county town. I'm new to it like you are, but we have shrunk everything to this small place.'

The husband was sitting with Henry Lowndes for coffee at the Cupola House restaurant a week or two later.

This Saturday morning proved conclusive. Henry was in his usual back room seat, surrounded by almost as much polished wood in the panelling as in his own furniture store rooms.

Today the tack would be different.

'Your father must have been glad of a son to take over?' was a decent enough opening the young man thought.

'It wasn't meant to be me, though. My older brother, Herbert, was killed in the War.'

'I'm sorry to hear that,' came the reply. 'Did he die in Germany?'

'No, it was in North Africa.' Henry paused. 'I was in Germany.'

Henry began pouring his second cup to reminisce. He hadn't been heard in this mode before.

'I went in late on, being the younger. I got to a good enough rank to be out of harm's way, but there was plenty to see.'

'Oh, yes?' came the reply.

'I wasn't even as old as you,' Henry continued, 'but I was sent from one Prisoner of War camp to another over the last year of the war. I was there to assess the value of the prisoners, and they were all in the high ranks, as it happened.'

'What a job,' the younger man replied. 'Demoralised, I suppose?'

'If that was the word for it. They were the worst of cowards. They bragged. They bragged about their lives before the war. It comes over, even in broken English, what wealth they had over the centuries and how they'd get back their position after the war.'

Henry drank up.

'I've got a few grandfather clocks at the back, you know.' He indicated towards Outgate with an incline of his head. 'Look at the names of the makers. All of them fine craftsmen from Austria, Germany, Switzerland. They turned their backs on all that to throw their killing rubbish at us, never mind what they did to Germans they chose not to think were worth the name.'

Henry sat back to relax. He put his hands in his lap.

The younger man stirred milk into his second cup.

'My wife enjoyed her visit to yours. She'll be at the shop now, Mrs. Lowndes, I suppose?'

'Yes,' said Henry. 'She likes her coffee mornings. I'd be here. She's there. She's got her ways.'

The reply was uneasy when it came.

'You must be glad to have company. She has a sweet tooth, collecting sugar tongs. The kids were fascinated.'

He spoke as he reached for the sugar on the table.

Henry Lowndes looked at the younger man, the able conversationalist, his following generation. Conversation could also be curt.

'I don't think I've told you about my first wife. We met at the end of the War.'

Henry looked at his spoon stirring round the cup.

'She was Jewish. She didn't take sugar. She was always quite sweet enough.'

# The Gilded Station

A high red-brick wall, a double gated entrance, an impressive three storeyed house in the fine local brick. Any county town possesses more than a few such edifices. Our history had made them a necessity.

This one, unimaginatively imposing and facing the chill east, was looking the wrong way. A windowless, grey, side wall fronted the roadway where three high steps lead to an unused servants' door.

To the south and west the gardens sprawled untidily up a slight rise from the main road. Vineyards once planted there had given the nearby abbey its coveted thin wine. Those who worked the soil wore black.

But soon the north gates would open to a Toy Museum.

A child saves up pocket money for toys at a local shop. A toy collector takes a cheque book a thousand miles or more. Locals passed the 'Sold' sign at the gate with no knowledge of this at all.

Colin Harwood had bought Stanhope House from a family which had lived there for fifty years. The French doors onto the garden had not been opened for a long time. The fitted carpets which had been removed by the previous owners revealed hidden uncared for floorboards at odds with the lightness of the uncurtained rooms. Outside, bootscrapers stood to attention beside the front door. Back and front sat uncomfortably in easterly afternoon sunlight, doubly friendless together. The front aspect welcomed the guest only to send him out of the doors to the same aspect, the only garden. Uphill, the sloping grounds did not invite, unless you were a child up for trees and rope ladders. Instead, wrought iron garden furniture of the better sort stood enticingly by a small pond and guests looked toward the house to find this garden simply by making a U-turn.

So it is with toys, Colin deliberated. As he bent down to his collection he knew he had entered his childhood's imaginative world of all those years ago, but he had exited again so as to look back at it with some chill in the air.

'Connie, just be careful with that particular box, won't you?' he called to his wife as the long, slow process of setting up began. 'That's the one with the track clips and pieces ready for the gilded station.'

Connie saw Colin as he spoke, not sharply but considerately to her. He was propped up on the kitchen sink having caught his breath and had seen her through the open door with that box.

'I'll let you have it now, dear,' said Connie, and she walked carefully towards him to hand it over.

Like many of the boxes they both unpacked that morning, this one was neither metric nor imperial, nor recognisable as a solid shoe box or loud hat box, but a squat square of grey card stapled at the corners quite unlike the everyday. It was a chocolate box shape devoid of wrapping and colour, so unenticing to the eye that it might contain a cramped tarantula, more than ready for the box the next size up. This is why collecting toys is a precarious pastime. Actions of the past have led to loss of parts for ever. Connie had watched Colin pack it up. With tweezers he carefully eased each small screw and even smaller washer into holes and spaces cut out of the inner cardboard. She knew Colin was quite right, that one tip and the contents would quite possibly be irretrievably unmatched. They might even slip between the staple and card to fall between floorboards and never be seen again.

Colin smiled with Connie at this collector's triumph. In so small a box was the result of months, Connie might say years, of painstaking attention to countless bits of toys, their screws, washers, plates, nuts, bolts, hinges and chains, a miniature shed's worth of minutiae for which the long drawn 'aah' of a find at auctions across Europe would, in a ratioed magnification, have been the loudest roar of a crowd at a rally.

They opened the box together. She held the bottom square gently with both hands and Colin put his on the top to carefully twist and jerk off the lid. Beside the sink, Colin laid the treasure down, saying with solemnity, 'Welcome. You are now housed in my new Museum.'

Connie patted her husband on the shoulder.

This enterprise was going to be unusual by any standard. The couple's three children were off their hands and away at University. Colin's new post at a local Dental Practice would begin in September. Stanhope House had been purchased in April and stood empty until this close July day. Connie was to help set up the exhibits with Colin while looking for a job in marketing to suit her experience. On top of all this, Colin had put himself forward as a local councilor to get known on the circuit.

All this was lost on the box, in fact on all the boxes of varied shapes and sizes now stacked in a morning room on the ground floor. Few of the boxes were large. Some were brightly coloured with a patina of advertising slogans, illustrations of the toy and maker's name. On the unpolished floorboards they toned in well, rather like a sepia photograph or an early colour film. They did not appear to stack comfortably, every toy being distinct and liking to think itself the favourite of every child called Johnny or Suzie, or Colin, if a collector came along.

Childhood is supposed to outlast the toy and not the toy the child, but, in this case, in the nuanced museum of childhood, the careful condition of each collected box seemed to confirm that the child had never used that toy or that the parent had shown it a more careful interest than the offspring. However it was, the usedness was a mask for a cautiously overhauled dream, a toy that would last for ever, into and beyond the perpetual innocence of the collector.

This was the perfect house for a home and a museum. The wide stairs in the hallway led up to two suites of rooms. The self-contained museum would be on the left, where there was a billiard room, for railways to be set in motion, with a doll gallery off, then a toy soldiers' room and a further annexe for boxed games and staring bears. The couple planned that the hallway would contain a small shop with books and merchandise and that, for visiting class groups, the garden would be for packed lunching while they waited for the coach to return them to school.

Colin's collection was ongoing. He travelled as often as he could to Toy Fairs across Europe. His knowledge was extensive. His face was familiar.

As Colin replaced the lid on the box, now placed next to the kitchen sink, he winked at Connie.

'Got a good one coming up to clinch it at last. I'm going over to Frankfurt on Friday and I'm hoping for a tip-off.'

'I'll get everything ready, dear,' said Connie encouragingly. She'd remembered where his best suit could be found. 'This could be it, then?'

'You bet. I'll get that gilded station one day soon, you'll see. I haven't been looking this long for nothing.'

'That's very true,' Connie replied, noting that the box was being placed carefully in a rucksack at Colin's feet. 'You'll be taking that onto the plane as hand luggage?'

'Oh, yes,' said Colin, looking up at his wife.

This was no new procedure for Connie. The grey box always went carefully on every trip to a Collectors' Fair. Who could know when the genuine article, the coveted gilded station, would turn up? In his half hour talks to school children Colin always mentioned his hunt for it.

'Why is it called the gilded station, Uncle Colin?' a nephew once asked.

'It's an unusually large station building, very grand really, and it's meant to clip in with tiny screws and brackets onto the exact base and platform which I've already got in my collection waiting for it. Only a rich German family would have bought it for their son. It's like an old-fashioned station building with chimneys, but it's got golden turrets at each of the four corners as well as a larger dome over the ticket hall in the middle,' was Colin's reply.

'Do you mean it might look like onion domes?' His questioner looked alert.

'Difficult to say. None of the toys I collect are from the Far East and not from the Middle East either, but let's say that when I find the gilded station it's likely to be in Eastern Germany or perhaps as far east as Poland. So, I'd expect the domes to be rounded with knobs on the top, not pointed like an onion.' replied Colin.

When Colin spoke to his wife he described a great deal more carefully. It was many years ago that he had said, 'Each dome would be good quality polished brass. They'd be highly lacquered and there mustn't be a blemish on any of them.'

'Would that really decrease the value?' Connie had asked.

'It's the trouble with brass, really. To glow like gold it can't have any tarnished patches. It'd take away from the coup it is, not just its value, to find a blemish.'

It had got to Friday at the end of a difficult week. The carpenter who had been booked in to fit the two sets of meandering shelving around the largest room to take the many model rail tracks, had come a day late. Colin had got angry.

'Damn the man! This is a fine-tuned business. It's not as if I can trust anyone but myself to get the track down and the stations set up.'

Connie came to help and all the boxes were in place when the carpenter had left. She had carried them up all by herself, but only Colin could set up.

'I can never tell which curved bit goes into which,' she said. 'I'd probably be all right on the straight.'

'Maybe,' said Colin, mollified by her helpfulness.

He set off on that Friday early. It was to be a long weekend only. He had far too much to do on return.

'Goodbye, dear,' said Connie, 'and good luck.'

She turned to get on with things.

Without Colin around, Connie could reach for her own thoughts more adequately. His collection so dominated the home as an issue of storage. Now, for the first time, with the mechanics of the move over and the collection around her set up as a contrasting world, she knew she'd take some adjusting to it.

She walked upstairs and hesitated before turning left. She'd seen these toys before, knew this collection back to front, knew other collectors and their wives but, just as Colin's absence made a space, this time an ache seemed to fill it.

She knew about toys. That much was simple; children play with them, but collecting toys as an adult was quite different. All parents play along with their children's toys. Debussy, the composer, has a popular piece inspired by playing with his daughter and her dolls, but collecting the outdated, the outmoded and then unloved toys might not be such a generous and artistic act of devotion. It might be devotion to a cause, but what exactly was the cause?

She shook her head firmly in order to tell herself that she'd no business psycho-analysing a good husband of twenty five years and decided to ring a friend, Jane.

'Jane, you're in. I'm so glad,' began Connie.

'Connie, it's you. I'd been hoping to hear. How have you been getting on with the tour-de-force? When can Peter and I come to see it set up?' she asked brightly.

'It's almost ready, Jane. We've had a heck of a time. Colin's just gone off to a Fair for the weekend.' Connie answered honestly.

'You are a Fair widow, then, aren't you?' laughed Jane. 'I get your drift. I'll come round for a coffee at eleven. All right?'

'Yes, see you,' said Connie and, returning the 'phone to the desk, went to the kitchen to prepare.

Upstairs, later, Jane was taken aback. 'I'd no idea it would look so impressive. He's never had this much out before, has he?'

'No, not by a long way,' said Connie. 'The carpenter was late and put us all behind. I rather wish he hadn't come at all.' Her tone made Jane look round.

'It won't be easy to go back on an idea like this, Connie. The entire room will be whirring with trains moving on the tracks and stopping at the stations. When the visitors tire of that they go off to the side rooms. That's the idea isn't it?' said Jane.

Connie nodded.

'I see, every train starts from here. It's so well planned,' Jane spoke cheerily thinking about Connie's oddly plummeting confidence. 'But it's not got a station on this platform yet. He hasn't got it finished.'

'That's the base for the gilded station Colin's always on about. It'll be the chief attraction as it's so rare and he's had a tip-off that he could find it at Frankfurt this weekend.'

'I see,' said Jane, who clearly hadn't been listening at various dinner parties. 'What sort of gold?'

'Oh, posh brass, Colin says, and to have no marks or rust, it's like looking for a needle in a haystack.' Connie rushed her words. She'd seen enough of Jane for the morning. 'I'll let you get back for lunch.'

On Sunday evening, Colin came in excitedly at about 6pm. He'd already contacted her about 'exciting finds', but then he always did that.

The sun was lingering almost faultlessly in the clear evening sky. A smell of a neighbour's barbecue came down the main road and over their high wall and didn't retreat when Colin closed the double wooden gates behind his car.

'You're safely back, Colin.' said Connie,' I hope you like this wine.'

She'd made an effort with canapés on the lawn and sat Colin down.

In the warm evening air, the car, fresh from its long trip from the airport, seemed to further hum with warmth.

'What have you got in the boot, then?' said Connie, holding her glass to clink at Colin's.

'Something that'll need more bubbly than this to celebrate,' Colin touched her hand on the metal table. 'I wanted to see your face as I told you. I've got the gilded station at last!' His face lit up, as did hers as he spoke.

'Well, you devil, keeping it from me,' said Connie and sipped a small amount of wine. 'Where was it all these years and could you afford it?'

'I knew you'd say that. I can, and I can sell some pieces to make up the shortfall. No problem.' Colin didn't take a drink from his glass. He continued purposefully.

'As to where I got it. It was at the Frankfurt Fair, of course, but it wasn't out on display, Connie, neither was it in the catalogue. I got to it by asking questions, lots of questions really.' As he spoke he took his wine glass, held it up to the blue sky and began to twist it round in the air before putting it down.

'But what's the reason for that?' urged Connie. 'You've never bought out of catalogue. What's the provenance? How can you prove anything on hearsay? It's not like you, Colin.'

Colin's reply was methodical, pause by pause, almost as if he was bent over the golden object with a tiny screwdriver, one by one twisting the screws and washers taken carefully from the grey box into place.

'It is a German piece. It's the right date and it's authentic. It's just what I want. It's in perfect condition, but no-one's saying it out loud in Germany. It's come over from Poland. It's been hidden for years. It's from Treblinka.'

At that word in her husband's reply, Connie seemed to catch the falling blackness of her mind in her hands and she looked firmly at Colin. It was as if she had been rehearsing her words for years when she said. 'That isn't coming out of the boot. That gilded station isn't coming into the Collection. That authenticity stinks!'

'Connie, it's only a toy,' said Colin.

'That's what you say, but it isn't true.' Connie spoke loudly now. 'It just isn't true.'

# Flower Ladies

It's too easy to imagine a woman named Bessie. What you might see is a dame, Pantomime or otherwise, big bosomed and rosy with equally expansive cheeks. You might, if you felt your sense of history secure, see a diminutive orphaned girl destined to be a scullery maid at the turn of the century. You'd be wrong about each stereotype, that trick of the mind's eye. Bessie had stood daily as a flower lady for over forty years in a certain part of London five miles from Covent Garden. Buxom she was, though not over-generous, and with just enough of well-fed cheeks to be rosy when the weather was chill. Her hair was black in the manner of a Bessie and she wore black; blouse, skirt and jumper. Her black apron had a large pocket. Flowers showed up best on a black background and flowers were her trade.

'Got no gladioli, lady. It ain't the season,'

Bessie spoke about what she hadn't got matter of factly but when it came to persuasion, she was unsurpassed.

Generations of flower girls had wheedled and cajoled as she did.

'You'll never get better bunches nowhere. These ain't market flowers. They're chose by me, fresh as daisies, and I choose the best for my customers.' she'd say convincingly and loudly.

You might well believe her. Around her ankles as she sat next to a large lamp post, were tall china pots which held her choices for the day. Fern curled around her knee, carnations in reds, whites and pinks peeped between. In Autumn, vast chrysanthemum heads in yellow and whites seemed to fill her lap and there was always Gypsophilia, the snowy flower filler of every bouquet or an airy lightener for the dread of a heavy task. Bessie knew about that.

She stood beside the wide, commanding gates of Abney Park Cemetery in North London. Almost all her trade was for the grave. She knew just how to sell her wares to those who entered those gates weekly, monthly, yearly. She recognised almost all of them.

Today it was, 'Mrs. Kent, 'allo, and what would you like this beautiful morning?'

Bessie greeted her well-known customer, about her own age.

It was March, a sharp day but promising.

'I'm going to have four of them white irises and a bit of fern with the Gyp you usually do for me, Bessie,' returned Mrs. Kent.

Bessie Barnham picked up the heads with a fancy flick, propelling the irises into her left hand deftly with the right. It was a trick of the wrist she had practised at Covent Garden. A good straight stem crossed strongly from the hand.

Mrs. Kent watched the woman's natural dexterity and said, 'How much are they coming up at today?'

'You know I'll give you a good price, Mrs. Kent. We've known each other a while.' She handed back a small amount of change with a 'Ta!'

It was thirty years ago she'd met Mrs. Kent, a couple of years before the war. Then, young Mrs. Bessie Barnham had a family of four to get to school and do for, so she learned the trade in the very early mornings at Covent Garden. Along with all the high-pitched voices and the shouting, Bessie got her technique up, sharpened her bargaining and was pleased that both her mother and father could see her into the trade. There was always a fall-back. Her husband Harry was on the Docks. They neither of them gave thought to tradition, nor could they know the changes the war would bring.

It was a faint memory now, but she was certain that the same lady had come up to her first on a cold day in April quite a few years ago. She had jet black hair, she remembered, just like herself, but she was thin, really quite thin. Her black jacket's broad shoulders, stiffened in the style then, looked drooped and hollowed. Her black eyes were lustreless. She didn't say much that time, or for the next few years, despite the weekly visits.

Bessie certainly didn't know her name. She was shy, despite the brightness which had come back into her eyes. Once she paid for two shilling's worth of flowers with threepenny bits, looking a bit awkward as she parted clumsily with the coins. They fell heavily into Bessie's apron, but were good for change at the time. Only at the outbreak of war did she open up a bit. Perhaps every Londoner did, Bessie thought. Mrs. Kent only came monthly then, and must have felt obliged to explain herself.

'I can't come as often as I did. I've got shift work at the 'Ever Ready', she said as she looked over the flowers.

'I'm sure your dad or mum'll forgive you for that,' said Bessie sympathetically. This large local Cemetery was very full.

'Oh, it's my kid in there; my first,' Mrs. Kent said, bending down to check a pale carnation. 'She died in the night. She hadn't even got to school age.'

'Oh my dearie dear,' said Bessie, caught short over that revelation. 'I don't see you when you come up with your husband on Sundays. Bert does this for me then. It's my day off.'

'Mr. Kent doesn't come. He's got War work and no mistake,' said the mother as she paid up and set off.

There was no mistake about the war. Then there came the night when a high impact bomb took a large block of flats and the air raid shelter below it. Almost two hundred men, women and children were killed in the raid.

It was a day or two after that tragedy when a gentleman came up to Bessie's small stall and began to look at the roses.

'How many would you like?' Bessie asked.

'Can you get me and my community fifty of them. We need them as a token for the victims of the bombing of Coronation Mansions. The Memorial gathering is planned for in here.' The gentleman indicated the Cemetery.

'Oh, I get you,' said Bessie, who couldn't phrase her response any better, just like anyone else in this close-knit Jewish neighbourhood where she worked her trade. Everyone had been shocked to the core.

'Can't tell you how sorry we all are for your people,' said Bessie, taking it upon herself to speak for the gentiles.

'Thanks, Bessie,' said the gentleman. 'Can you do that number then?'

'I'm positive for Friday morning,' Bessie replied. 'All right?'

Bessie and a good many others were there for the Friday lunchtime committal. A great many black hats bobbed together on the Jewish menfolk as they stood in groups across the road. Fifty other young men, each dressed in black suits but with a cream scarf hanging loosely down to their waists, lined the wide entrance to the Cemetery.

Bessie was in a good position and saw the local Councillors, the Mayor, the MP, the Borough Council workers who'd seen to the tragedy and who had dug down through the mass of bricks to the shelter beneath, all gathered round. Then she spotted Mrs. Kent. The man standing beside her was tall with dark hair; Mr. Kent evidently. What she did not know was that he had led the men who went in to take out the bodies. The local papers said it was a gruesome business.

'War is,' thought Bessie, 'and good for business,' she said glumly to herself.

That particular lunchtime she looked at Mr. and Mrs. Kent again more carefully. There were no kids near them.

Bessie found time to go into the Cemetery the next week to find the spot chosen for the Memorial. The fund had been set up.

That morning Bessie set up a few pots to mark that she was about, then she turned in through the gates. She had her cash in her apron.

There always seemed to be a mist in this vast green and grey place. The foliage made it sweat, she knew. She walked past the opening circle of benches set back around a wide bed of geraniums and then turned off to the left. This was a place to be easily lost. She was used to giving directions to customers.

She found the spot. It had been cleared quite thoroughly and there were the rose stems all around what was to be the memorial space. Bessie moved closer, thinking of her day's flowers hidden up by the gate, but determined to have her look like so many others over the last week. Then she noticed that the Council had pinned up a book of names on a post beside the circle of roses. It was a block book, quarto sized and looped by thin wire on to a thick, curved nail. She wasn't sure she wanted to look, but opened at the first page nevertheless. The pages were typed; name, age and number of the flat. This must have come from the Council records. She went over a few pages.

'Blimey! Barthold, Bernstein, Bronowsky.' she spoke out loud before putting the book carefully down against its post.

'Mustn't forget'em. No, we mustn't,' she spoke angrily on her way back to the entrance. 'No-one's forgotten in here.'

A couple or years later, or she thought it was, the easily recognised, black-haired Mrs. Kent came up to her small stall. She was carrying a shopping bag held close to her front.

''Allo! How are you, then?' said Bessie, who noted a few grey hairs among the black ones. She'd been counting her own only that morning.

'I'm all right, Bessie, thanks.' said Mrs. Kent, then, 'I'll have daffs today. They really are bright.'

She paid and went off carrying the daffodils high up near her waist.

Bessie could not have more clearly remembered the next time Mrs. Kent came to the stall.

'Oh, my goodness, look at you!' Bessie spoke in sharp surprise.

It was close to Christmas. Mrs. Kent came round the sweeping corner of the Cemetery entrance with a dark blue twin pram. Both hoods were up.

'Where did they come from? What have you got, you dark horse?'

She peeped in, dazzled by bright white, knitted bonnets.

'Two girls, aah. What do you call them?' Bessie was delighted for her customer of so many years.

'This one's Helen and this one's Marjorie', said Mrs. Kent proudly, hingeing the pram hoods down so that Bessie could see the black-haired babies of six months.

'In wartime, too. That'll cheer you up. God knows when it'll end.' Bessie's ready smile was truly intended to bring the end closer, you would think.

''Specially me, as long as they don't evacuate us', said the mother. She bent down to look at how much the chrysanthemums cost, saying 'I've had two for the price of one.' Then, 'I'll try these,' and she pointed to the golden bronze. 'I'll have three of the largest, and could you cut them shorter for my vase? They're strong blooms.'

'Right you are, dear,' replied Bessie.

This was the way of the world. Business as usual was all right with her.

She got no more business from Mrs. Kent for a while and rather misssed her about. She put it down to having twins at her age, and it meant that Bessie was very nearly knocked off her small stool with surprise one Saturday a couple of years later.

'What's this then?' Bessie actually stood up to greet the small procession coming round the corner.

Mrs. Kent was well wrapped up against the Christmas chill in a winter coat and headscarf. Her two lively identical twin girls had light blue woollen coats with reins round each of them. They were looped onto each side of a single pram. The hood didn't hide the baby sitting up inside.

Mrs. Kent came slowly on and a smile came to her face when she saw Bessie standing. She answered.

'This is my next one. I've got another girl. She's nearly a year now.'

'She's a lovely. What d'you call her?' asked Bessie.

'Rose. I've given her a flower name.' Mrs. Kent untied Rose's bonnet as she spoke, to reveal a mass of light brown curls.

'Well, you are a wonder,' said Bessie, returning to her seat. 'How on earth did you get down the High Street with all this?'

'Mr. Kent's off work this afternoon. He came with us. He won't be too long in the pub,' said Mrs. Kent and she went on to chat to the two girls who were touching the flowers.

'Shall we have red or yellow today?' she said to them both. 'We're going to take some flowers in here.'

Their mother pointed to the Cemetery gates.

Bessie looked up at Mrs. Kent as she pulled out a half crown to pay.

'It'll be a playground for them in there,' she said quietly.

Bessie watched the Kent family grow up and go to Primary School. After that she only sat on the job at weekends. One of her sons did the quieter week days and opened a corner florists over the road. His pots were plastic. It was better to have the business close by with the Docks changing so much. Most of those in the locality had no more memory of a flower lady than they had of the war, thought Bessie.

One day, long after the regular visits to Abney Cemetery had ceased, Mrs. Kent came into the florist shop to ask for her.

'Mum'll be pleased with your order, Mrs. Kent. It sounds like it's for old times' sake. Thanks a lot for using us,' said Ken Barnham, a large man of about forty. 'I'll get her to come and chat it over with you. Will next Monday be all right?'

On that day the two women met. Mrs. Kent had a smart, glossy brochure handed to her, but instead she looked at Bessie the Flower Lady.

'Bessie, the Wedding flowers for Helen have got to be the best you can do, like you've always done for me. Mr. Kent's been passed on a year now, but he'd say the same as me. Only the best for our oldest girl.'

''Course I will, love,' said Bessie, taking the coloured brochure from her. 'And you'll want white, I know.'

'Yes, all white. Can you make it as many types of small white flowers as you can. I suppose white roses are pricey?' said Mrs. Kent.

'Well, 'course they are, but you couldn't do without some. I'll give you a special price on those,' replied Bessie.

What slim plans that were made went ahead for the wedding at the local church. The flowers arrived at Mrs. Kent's flat in the early morning, delivered by Bessie's son.

Ellen Kent looked at Bessie's posies, tightly budded and placed alongside each other on the side table. Creams, whites, pale yellows, a hint of palest green with the bride's bouquet trailing delicately almost to the floor. How did the lady in black find so many white flowers?

Just for a moment the mother saw them on Meg's grave, covering its small stone completely, that little mound swathed in white. Then suddenly Helen came into the sitting room and decided to whoop for her sisters. They came up behind her from the bedroom, crowding over by their mother to catch up their bridesmaids bouquets eagerly. Helen raised hers high and her two sisters did the same.

'It's our day, Mum,' cried Helen, hugging her mother. 'All your daughters are together! I've never seen such beautiful white flowers. Thank you!'

# The Drawer

A small stool with very uneven legs stood beside the over-large drawer in the workshed at the bottom of the garden. Dad had told him he could be there after school, which left about an hour before he got in from work. He wasn't to be there at weekends.

Ben had an hour to himself just about every day because his older brother had recently started a first job. Ben was ten and had always been too far from Will in age to be a crony, nor yet near enough to be an enemy. The distance was just right, both sensed. They could get on alone.

'I'm going down the shed, Mum,' called Ben from the back door.

'Okay, Ben. We'll catch up with dad later,' he heard her faintly reply.

Ben knew there was nothing special about the back door, the path to the shed or even the shed, but the drawer was different. First of all it didn't fit the drawer space and was stuck at just under halfway out, as if two arguing carpenters had made a pact. Even the stool in front of it argued in the way it lurched forward, then dipped backwards never at the split second you expected of it.

Each centimetre out of kilter fired Ben. He could think about it for ages, even lying in bed, but especially in maths lessons. Why didn't things match up?

'Dad, I've found sixteen hinges in the drawer. Where do they come from?' said Ben to his father that same early evening.

'I don't know, Ben,' his father said grumpily that day. He'd had another argument with Will that morning. At sixteen and just out to work, Will was finding his feet in a way his father didn't altogether like. But he continued, 'What on earth did you count them all out for? I hope you're washing your hands before supper.'

'Yes, dad,' replied Ben and ran up to the bathroom to do so. Will came out of his bedroom and met him at the top of the narrow stairs.

'Dad got you scared, has he?' Will sneered.

Ben ducked under his restraining arm and went to the bathroom.

'It's liver and bacon for supper,' he said.

Downstairs, on a small square table in the sitting room, four places were set for the family. As Ben was coming down the stairs, he heard mother serving up and Dad and Will just about to begin a set to.

'You ought not to have done that, dad,' Will said pensively and his father replied, 'Well, I've done it and that's that,' when his mother shouted out, 'It's all ready and don't you two even think of arguing now!'

Ben hurried into the room to sit down. Will turned to him.

'I'm all day at work now and what do you get up to in that shed? At least it keeps you out of the way,' he said.

'Oh, I don't do much. It's just interesting, that's all.' Ben's reply was rushed and he was pleased to see his mother with the plates of food.

'Charlie Newham doesn't get as much as this every day, Mum. He was telling me at playtime that his dad gets the best food or else, and he gets a bit of fish,' he said, picking up his knife and fork.

'Fair's fair in this house, son,' said his father and looked at Will as he said it. 'I blame a weak woman. 'Course the kids need their food.'

'Well, I'm paying plenty for mine now,' said Will.

'Yes, you are, Will,' said his mother, 'and look how much you eat.'

The meal continued. Will glared at his brother.

Next day was a Friday and the end of a decent week at school for Ben. His friends left him to walk home calling, 'See you down at the patch,' which was the local playing field close to the river.

Ben called back purposefully. 'Yes, I might.' and all seemed well. He wondered what was for tea.

Ben rounded the corner of the lane which ran down the side of the long garden of his home. The fence was not kept up very well on the lane side, only well enough, said dad, so he didn't get a letter about it, but didn't have to pay a fortune on the upkeep of it.

Ben looked at the shed roof as he turned. It was on a busy corner, really, but was so quiet inside.

'It's because it's at the end of a nice, long garden,' he thought, looking forward to his hour in there.

The sound of every hinge is different. Ben's ears caught the metallic creak of the front gate, the near noiseless smoothness of the front door and the squeak of the kitchen door.

'Hello, Mum. I'm home and I'll be down at the bottom, all right?' He craned his head in. Mum was at the sink.

'All right, Ben, and don't overstay your time tonight. Your dad and I are going out for a few hours and I want you out of there and had your tea by six.' She sounded pleased he thought.

Down at the shed, which had a sliding door, Ben jumped in and got down to rummaging. The door stayed open, but not to give light. It was just that the long garden made Ben feel he was quite distant enough. Light came through a wide, high up window on the south side. The drawer was under the window.

Today he was going for corks and bottle tops. Ben sat on the stool and lurched towards his playground, the drawer. It contained everything kept for another day by a working man with a working life at home, and possibly everything from his father, too. Every spare nail, screw and bolt from every job or strip down. It was the flotsam and jetsam of so many repeat remarks. 'That'll be useful one day.' If Ben sat at the centre and put his arms out wide, the drawer's width was equal both sides at his elbows. In fact, he often sat with elbows bent in, leaning on the wooden edge peering down into the drawer, breathing heavily and smelling the oil, greasy dirt, gummy string and leaks of old glue. He pulled the near open drawer towards him on to his knees as far as was safe and sat comfortably to begin.

Ben's method was to turn over a corner into the centre, so, beginning top end left, he scooped up the depth of bits and pieces, overhauling them like an excited trainee archaeologist, forgetting to examine and just revelling in the slide and slither of screw upon bolt, nail upon washer, peg upon pipe. It felt like mining for gold. It was certainly not one nugget which spurred the search, no, it was the everything of it all, each new item at every turn of the pile and fall of the pieces. Gradually, Ben's finds built up. He tried to memorise each static moment of the pile before it fell, mentally photographing the position of every clip, tiny canister, steel shaft and spring so as to refine his search next time. He was seeing the brass hooks which caught things up and shouldn't have; a washer dangling, a rubber band caught, a spring skewered, a cork tightly wedged and he waved them in the air as a catch, watching the small appendages shake back into his drawer. His was the enquiring mind, settling a pattern and patterning in the search.

He found fourteen bottle caps, mostly dark green, and twenty corks, most of them long and thin.

'Pop gun size,' he thought, thinking of dad at his age long, long ago.

'Time to go.' Ben hurried off his seat, the seat which always threw him backwards abruptly with that thought, and he set off down the garden path. He heard bikes in the lane. Workers coming home.

'I'm all right for time, then,' he thought.

'They're not here, yet,' said his mother as he came into the kitchen, 'so you're all right.' She eyed her son fondly. 'You've done well at school all week, I hope?'

'Yes, mum,' said Ben. 'I came second in spelling this week, but I'll come top next, you'll see.'

'See you wash your hands first,' said his mother.

It was only fifteen minutes later that the meal was under way and Will was saying, 'I'll be in tonight, Mum.'

'Oh, then Ben'll be all right, won't you, Ben? We'll be home before dark.' His Mum looked at her husband.

'What you doing then, Will?' said his father, giving him a sideways glance.

'Oh, this and that,' he replied. 'I'll be in my room.'

Ben was enjoying his fish pie. He loved the mash. He began to make it into swirls on his plate, running his fork through for evenly spaced parallel wavy lines.

'Where do you think you are, at the seaside?' said Will, so as not to meet his father's gaze.

'Eat up properly, Ben. We've got to get out,' said his mother and got up to go to the kitchen for dessert.

'I'll be all right down the shed, won't I, dad?' said Ben, scooping up the thin layers of mash. 'I'm on the lookout for corks.'

'There'll be a good few and very useful they are, too. If you can find a box you can keep them all together,' said his father.

'Might do, dad,' said Ben and finished his course quickly so as to be ready for apple pie.

Later, looking out for dad to ask about going down to the patch the next day, he heard his mother say, 'He's got the run of the house. You're sure you put it safely away?'

'Yes, of course I did, Beryl,' his father replied.

Ben got his go-ahead on the patch and walked off down the garden path.

It was a simple garden, none too wide. Grass near the house held the washing line above the kick-a-ball-about area. Then came the vegetable garden, both sides of the path, carefully laid out. After that were raspberry canes, then the shed.

Ben's mid-summer evening was assured. He took a wooden tray down from the shelf, removing the plant pots, and began his new task of hunting for two inch cross cut screws. He loved the clean-cut look of them.

'Dad must have unscrewed a wardrobe or something big for this lot.' They grouped on his tray a gleaming, satisfying hoard. His search continued.

Ben was just beginning to feel happy about his collection when he heard a popping sound up near the house. He felt uneasy immediately. He'd heard the sound before for just a couple of nights about two weeks ago. Then it had been Will's new air rifle. Mum and Dad had been very angry with him, because he'd exchanged it for the bike he'd got at Christmas ready for the new job in June.

Dad's voice had been raised and Mum had been pleading. Then there wasn't the gun any more, neither was there a bicycle.

The popping continued. There were equal intervals and a purposefulness to it.

'It must be Will practising on the lane fence, like he did before, but how did the gun get back?'

Ben thought carefully. Then he remembered that Mum and Dad were out.

He put back the drawer, balancing his tray as he did so, slid off the tilting stool before putting the tray to one side and went to the open door. Stepping through he heard the poppings continue methodically but couldn't see his brother. As he moved down the path, Ben heard voices in the lane, boy's voices. They sounded young, younger than him anyway. They were making their way home.

He heard them talking.

'Bet you can't,' said one.

'Yes, I can you know. Mum says. Hang on, what's that over the fence?' said his friend.

'I'll see,' came the reply, then came screams carried over the fence on the cooler evening air.

Ben ran down past the vegetables and on to the grass to find Will sitting down as if he had just been pushed over. The air gun was beside him. He looked up at Ben with a face of terrible fear.

'How could I have hit anyone through the fence?' His voice sounded so thick it was difficult to hear him.

Voices came from over the fence now. Neighbours and passers by were calling out.

Then came a strident voice. 'Come out and see what you've done!' followed by a banging on the fence.

A knock came on the front door and Will got to his feet. He went through the back door, past the kitchen and hall in that straight line of doors. Ben could easily see who was there.

A tall man was silhouetted in front of Will. Ben saw that he had his shirt sleeves rolled up.

'Have you been in your garden? What've you been playing at?' Ben heard him say from where he was standing by the rifle on the grass.

'You'd better come through,' Ben heard Will say and then the man came through into the garden.

He spoke cautiously when he saw Ben.

'He went to look through a hole in your fence, like he shouldn't have, but he did, and look what's happened. It's gone right into his eye. The ambulance is coming.'

Will and the man went back into the house and Ben was left. The fuss in the lane went on, but the boys were quietened by grown-ups. Ben went in and upstairs to his bedroom, where he sat on the bed unable to move. His brother had shot a boy in the eye through the fence. How could it have happened?

Mum came up after about an hour to say, 'Stay here, Ben, and get into bed. We'll talk about it in the morning, when we know how the little boy is.' Mum didn't look like Mum.

Next morning, what words came conveyed the truth that his brother had been searching in the house that evening for the confiscated air rifle. Will found it in his parents' bedroom and brought it down to the garden to shoot. The worn fence had quite a few holes in it, but how was he to know that a little boy would choose a peep hole at the exact moment he aimed?

That evening Mum put a plate of two fried eggs in front of Ben.

'Will's upstairs with your dad. Eat up,' she said.

'He must have found it in a drawer then, Mum?' Ben didn't know whether to pick up knife or fork first. He felt lopsided.

'Yes, he did,' said his mum.

# Number 48

Winter was about to close in. Marika knew it because, along with the small twigs dropping on to the great wide lawn, there were tiny flakes of snow clinging to the thinnest of them to aid their descent.

Standing at the top of the grand stairs, Marika saw the gardener in the distance through the long window carrying a sack over his shoulder. He had probably been out by the lake to collect cones. They made a lovely crackle on the hearth, bringing the warmth of a cold land from their own woods. Marika could not shout to Peotr through the window, but she wanted to do so. Mama and Papa had been out with the pony and trap since just before noon and it was now mid-afternoon, becoming misty in the manner of all winter days ending in this part of Europe.

Marika turned back into the house and its corridors to fetch her coat and hat. Downstairs she would pull on her boots then try to find Peotr as someone to talk to. The two other servants had the half day off and Marika was unused to being alone. After lunch, the aloneness had wrapped her up as firmly as her fur coat, and she desperately wanted the only two she loved to unbutton the cloak, just as they did a fortnight ago on her fifteenth birthday when they went for a family drive in the trap around their grounds.

'You are just dipping your toes into the water, luby Marika,' said her mother, 'and who knows how soon you'll be able to swim.'

It was as she was pulling on her boots in the side room off the scullery that Marika heard the distant barking of dogs.

'Don't do that! Don't do that!' Shouting echoed from around the far side of the house.

Marika crouched down in a position she had never used before, like a dog about to back away from a lead.

111

A voice she knew well was speaking loudly and clearly.

'There's no-one in. They're all gone out on a ride. There's no-one in at all.' Peotr was shouting and the crispness in the mist made it all too clear why his voice was raised.

As the meaning of the sound came to Marika's ears, she carefully edged forward to find a cupboard.

She tried to piece the noises together. Who would be about as dusk was falling? Where were mama and papa?

Russian soldiers use back doors. They burst in and found a tearful young girl in a cream coat with fur at the neck, cuffs and hem standing by a bucket of potato peelings by the scullery cupboard.

'That's not a job for you.' they sneered at her. 'You, young lady, whoever you are, are coming with us.'

Marika told this story many times in the cold winter of 1939. Basha listened dispassionately.

'My parents went off on a different train. You and me were sent to the sewing circle,' she grimaced, looking at the large bodkin in her hand. Every girl guarded their own.

'Shed 48 could be a lot worse,' said Marika to Basha, 'Some of them have got treadmills. At least we've got hand sewing machines.'

The short break ended and guards were wandering back in from a smoke outside.

The young women of Shed number 48 made a good many items of uniform, clothing their own captors against the bitterness of a Siberian winter.

'Russian soldiers don't dress as well as our young men,' whispered Basha, determined to say a little more about home. 'Polish soldiers keep the creases.'

Marika decided not to nod, although she would have vigorously done so. Basha's father was in the Polish army. She was a Barracks girl by upbringing. It wasn't safe to be open with gestures, she had indicated to Marika.

Marika's airy home seemed as far away to her now as would Basha's Barracks have seemed after nine months in this tormenting place. Now she was surrounded by wasteland for hundreds of kilometres, by forests of alarming depth and watery inland lagoons reflecting the same endless grey sky which made them. A slow, packed train passed them, shuttling Poles even deeper into this terror of a region, Siberia.

The girls went back to the long rows of sewing tables and sat up on stools to bend over their machines. Grey faced, grey eyed, their sunshine-fair hair dirty and wisping under their rough blue caps, the workers could be said to appear as serene as scowls of concentration made them.

'When the War is over, you can go home, but it's all ours now. We've got your homeland now,' they were told often enough by their guards.

At eighteen years old, Marika's life was startlingly the same as when she came; the job laborious, the company lacklustre and sleep denied in the long, worrying, cold winter nights.

That summer, however, there was a change. The guards were fewer and they were older. No-one knew why. If there was a problem with the War they were not told, but at last Marika dared to put her dream into words.

'Let's get out,' she said to Basha urgently one day. There was no need to say why, only how. 'Shed 48 isn't guarded like it was, so we've got a chance after dark. Halina and Jolanta have said they'll double back as the women are counted out at 6pm, so we're not missed, then it's the back door of the shed and over the high wall.'

Basha's agreement was to wave her bodkin in the air for a moment.

There was nothing the two young women could take. They managed the wall, rubbed their torn knees, then slipped into the surrounding forest like wild animals do, seeking woodland cover. Green leaves, small and perfectly formed, grew above their heads as they walked on silently, each busy with fears of their own. They moved south and west making for a safe place. A Russian village, the Polish border? How could they know what was safe? It was not even safe to talk, only to walk.

113

The first few days were dry, then in a cooling light rain, the two young women skirted the perimeter of a very small farm. It was abandoned, they knew, because no dogs barked. Marika pointed out the vegetable garden.

'It'll give us something to carry on with.' she said.

The two of them were almost gleeful at finding raspberry canes with fruit nearly ripe. They sat to eat in the long grass. It was not the only time. Seeds, berries, pods, fungi, were their diet. The Polish girl from the big house who had dallied round the estate with the gardeners when she was young had learned what there was to eat in season. Marika knew what was what. She and Basha had picked and foraged all the way to this fruit-filled patch.

Young as they were, the journey wearied them more than they knew.

'I just want to find a friendly face,' said Marika one night, thinking of Peotr and his warning call, 'There's no-one here,' from that Polish afternoon so long ago. It was just like that as they camped up in a pine wood after three weeks. There was no-one here, yet.

'We might know what friendly is, but we might not,' said Basha.

She and Marika told their tale to the driver of a Red Cross van. They found the empty, broken down vehicle at a roadside and kept watch for movement. There were nuts in abundance in the nearby wood that September, but they chilled the fingers when picked up from the soil. Frosts would come very soon.

Marika and Basha had watched the driver when he returned to the van with a can of water earlier. He was not Russian because he kicked his van saying, 'Du er en dum maskine!'

He immediately spoke to them as they came out of the wood together.

'Polish?' he said gruffly, then, 'Get in the back.'

The van set off to catch up with a convoy travelling South from checks on Prisoner of War Camps. Marika's English, learned from her Belgian mother, was to be good enough for the journey, the long explanations at the Base, the form filling and the blissful 'aah' of a bath.

Again and again Marika told her story to different escorts on the move, by train, by truck and by pony.

Basha was to go West to Switzerland. Marika went from the first town beyond the Ural Mountains on to Grozny by rail and road, then on to Tehran. She was bound for South Africa.

On board her first big cargo boat she gazed at the sea swirling at the bows, anxious to shout out above its gurgling insistence. But the sea could no more answer her questions than the grown up woman she found herself to be, now eighteen and going farther and farther away from home. Her parents only knew her as a girl. Would they know this woman, straining now to see every bird, wishing it would take her love to them? She leaned towards the greyness of the sea to reach that grey mist which had taken her from them then. She pulled her coat round her.

The long voyage over, Marika would tell her outlandish story in Cape Town, the safest of havens.

'Marika, isn't it?' said the Royal Air Force desk man. 'I can't be expected to pronounce the next bit. You've got some voluntary work with us at weekends in the canteen. I see you're a typist all the week?'

'Yes, I am,' said Marika proudly. For a year she'd been indispensable at the High Commission pool. Fluent in Russian, Polish, German and English as she was, some important queries came her way.

'We've got Poles here on the base. Most of them are airmen and damn good they are. I don't need to tell you to watch out for them, do I?' He smiled at her under a moustache the exact grey of his hair. 'You can look after yourself.'

It was a few months later that a tall airman came up to the bar.

'Marika? That's a nice name.' he said.

She was glad of the uniform apron which covered a thin and worn blouse. Her thick fair hair was shoulder length now and was held back with a wide clip to spread it like a fan at the back of her head. A perky cap sat balanced on the side parting curls. Her full cheeks had a little more colour as she replied, 'I'm glad you think so.'

In a place where many nationalities met and many stories were exchanged and distorted, her tale was one of hundreds to tell, but Marika did not look back from that cheeky introduction.

'Dance tonight, Marika?' and, 'Join me for a drink this side of the counter?' and then, 'How come we're getting on so well?' Finally, 'The boys say we've got to hitch. Will you marry me?'

Gerry was stationed in South Africa as part of the British Squadron there. He had been in the Foreign Legion, he had been at Tobruk. His German surname meant whatever you wanted it to mean in Cape Town. He was proud of it and Marika had her man and his name.

When their two children arrived, Marika wanted them to be unaware of the vastness in the past of both parents. The present was too exciting. Their upbringing in the RAF took them nearly as far as Marika had travelled in her journey to safety. They were in Singapore, Hong Kong and other bases in the Far East, and always backwards and forwards by air to Boarding Schools in England.

These were the hostess years of flower arranging, napkin folding and an Officers' Mess life like a black and white film of the era we can all imagine. Gerry and Marika collected items from the East, made friends and contacts, made 'phone calls to England. Marika spoke very little about the war, distancing others as well as herself from the tearing inhumanity of the time.

'Just pack your bag yourself, William,' Tom said to his son. 'We'll soon be back in England and then you won't need to pack at all,'

'Make your last term a good one, Christie, and get some really good marks,' said Marika to her daughter.

'Suffolk sounds a small place after Singapore,' said Gerry when the teenagers had left the lounge. 'I'll see to it that I have one of the best houses on the Base for you, Marika.'

'I'm sure you will, Gerry,' obligingly replied the once homeless, rootless Marika after twenty years of married life in a Crown Colony.

Marika's tales of Singapore served as dinner party conversation for the next fifteen years in England. Entertaining was at the forefront of her life. It was as if the foraging for months in an angry landscape made her into the wife whose presentation had to be impeccable. Marika made a show and was feted for it. She found there was a smart cook at her core. Gerry chose the fine wine. Marika set her table with cut crystal bowls and fluted glasses with a rainbow glint all in orderly fashion beside the plates. She took these bold colours as themes for the flower arrangements. They were stiff, upright and tidy as the style of the decade dictated.

At sixteen, Marika would have blushingly joined her parents at relaxed evening dinners with cultivated friends, expected to converse and become part of a society which shone brightly across Europe, but the sun went down. Short-changed, Siberia saw little of its rays. Marika's new life brightened others, and if style, as some think, is a form of excess, they did not know of her story.

No wonder, then, that the home for their retirement away from the Norfolk Base had to be substantial, detached and in a leafy road close to the many friends they had made. The house seemed to suit from every brochure angle and the two of them drove over to look.

Marika stepped out of Gerry's Mercedes in a three-quarter fur coat and smart black trousers. She saw the number on the gate but instead of walking towards this most promising purchase, she turned along the road to the neighbouring house. The car door had been left open. The gate to the house stood shut. Gerry quickened his pace after her. He guided his wife by the elbow back to the car. He shut its door and turned to open the gate to number 49.

'Don't worry, Marika,' he said, looking at her face. 'I've checked. It's not over the road and it's not next door. House number 48 isn't here.'

# 1881: The Census Speaks

'Eveline, it's a long way to go for work,' said Mrs. Maynard. 'Your father and I would love to have you a bit closer to us than York. What a journey.'

'I'll manage, Mother. I really don't want you to worry about the distance. It's the job which counts, and it's a good one.'

Eveline adjusted the waistband of her long navy skirt, pulling the front seam to the centre. It was a thick wool and had been bought in Tuckers in Northampton. York would be just the same as Northampton she judged while she was in the shop feeling very excited by the grown-up purchase.

'Dad, it's not the most expensive, but it isn't cheap,' she'd said as he paid up the two shillings.

'This is lady's money,' he'd said tersely as he turned. 'It's you the maid as is spending all mine.'

Eveline had given her father a squeeze of his arm as they left the shop.

'It'll all be worth it,' she'd said. 'I know I'll do well up there.'

Their village was named Cold Higham with good reason. It was a windswept spot on the Northamptonshire uplands and couldn't be called secluded, but its good-looking cottages were well-kept. Their snug fires had been centrepieces for generations. They were hearths worn away by slumped figures waiting for supper and the feet of children fidgeting to keep warm. The fireplace saw activity on every moonless winter night and bright spring morning when the wind circled the fields and nipped at sleeping trees or their new leaf buds. A long Roman road lay alongside the comfortable busyness of the village, but few knew that Watling Street had seen bustle they could scarce imagine.

East Yorkshire was equally exposed to upland wind. Draughts of sea-pure chill air blew into Compton Agnes, swirling with the breezes of the Wolds, seemingly centring on the Hall named after its village. It stood not too far from the main road to the sea at Bridlington with its parkland largely laid out up and behind it to meet the wind from which it sheltered in surroundings of formal beds and kitchen garden wall.

'Get off that chair, you silly bitch!'

There wasn't any need for this to be said to the old dog, but Molly had been his mother's before she left Compton Agnes, and any affection had gone with her.

'Arnold, that's uncalled for,' said his wife, Phyllida. She reached for the marmalade spoon, then glanced at him and down at her morning dress.

'Do you like this shade of cream? It's just a change from lavender. Adrianna Talbot will call this morning.'

'Don't give her my love,' replied her husband and rustled the paper between them. 'But enjoy things while I'm away in York. I expect to be on my way by Wednesday and will break my journey at Driffield. There are a few arrangements to confirm before the month of the Fair.'

Eveline didn't have days off in the new job, let alone months to amble strangely winding streets and acquaint herself with York. From the garden of The Mount House she could see the Minster tower in all weathers and lights and, on her half day, she would walk down to the Bar. She 'poked around' in the old city as she wrote to her father and mother. It wasn't at all like Northampton.

Dowager Lady Benyon made herself available on Eveline's first day. She was in the Drawing Room and standing by the window which looked out on the road.

'Come in. Eveline Maynard, isn't it?'

Eveline moved on into the room and saw the elderly figure of her employer against the spring sunshine urging itself into the room through a tall bay window. The view showed a recently planted tree coming into leaf on the road side. Eveline saw the newly-built stone house at a distance opposite and wondered at the servants there, all before answering.

'Yes, your Ladyship. I'm Eveline.'

'I'm glad you're here and are ready to begin. Has Dawson shown you everything?'

'Yes, your Ladyship,' replied Eveline.

'I'll have tea now, and I'll call you Evie,' said Lady Benyon and she came from the window. As she approached, colour came from the shadows in the folds of her dress. Light mauves and cherry pinks were muted with a heavy beige lace. The dress rustled like a fully leaved tree in the nip of a wind as Eveline waited for further instructions.

'Just Breakfast blend, Evie, and a shortbread.'

Eveline nodded, bobbed and retreated.

'She don't usually ask for tea this early, Eveline, but when Sir Arnold's visiting York on business, she's always in a flap well before he comes.'

Eveline's morning off that first week coincided with a breaking cloudscape over the Bar as she walked down Mount Road. It was quiet, with only raucous birds paying attention to new shoots on the bushes hedging the well-paved drives. As she came to the end of Blossom Street and closer to Micklegate Bar, there were terraced houses and a 'selection', her father termed it that in Northampton, 'of residents'. As the sun broke through over the Bar there was no warmth for Eveline because she was passing the Convent wall which shaded the narrow road all day. Once inside the old walls of the town, there was a more varied play of sun and shade, so Eveline felt quite at home. Across the fields around her family home there was an insistent play of clouds. Long shadows followed the footpaths there and were firm friends with each tree. They had made a wider welcome year by year to her lengthening legs and arms. She could not see up to the crown and judge the growth as a bird might.

'How grounded thoughts are to a child,' she smiled, 'when each large pebble is a milestone.'

She had got up and along almost to the Minster, walking up the hill and not watching her feet. There she was going to halt. Eveline had never seen a Church so large before and the walk around it confirmed her impressions of a giant stone frame and acres of black glass. She debated whether it would be hot or cold. This eighteen year-old decided it would be warm with cold, draughty corners, like the Church at home.

She was back at The Mount well before her allotted time and found Mrs. Dawson had laid a cold luncheon already.

'I'm getting ahead, Eveline, because Sir Arnold is coming in a couple of weeks.'


'What horses have we got, Messenger?'

Sir Arnold Benyon spoke to his ostler.

'Darnley, m'Lord, and his daughter, 'Braver Lady', d'you mean?'

'I do and I don't. I want names for the Fair, Messenger, and a way forward for it.'

'Gross'll look after everything, as usual, m'Lord. Are you settled as to which day you will attend?'

'Yes, I am. It's a way ahead, but I am confirming a few matters in Driffield over the coming week. I'm going over with James Cartaret, a gentleman from Bridlington.'

Sir Arnold paced across the stable yard where Messenger heard him coughing quite as much as his horses.

Cartaret was to drive him over to York next week and there was a substantial amount to get on with. He glanced up the rooks cawing in the lime trees of the drive. It was messy twig time for them as they re-lined their wind-riding domains. He peevishly kicked a few large twigs lying around the stables but he didn't look up again. Instead, he looked down at his boots. Would mother disapprove of his expenditure? He didn't care a damn if she did.


After her lunch, Eveline had time to look over the house before Lady Benyon would call for tea. She went to her room to change and met Stanton on her way up. He was gardener and odd-job man and he was at the turn in the stairs in front of a door which opened onto a wide linen room.

'It's catching, this door, Miss Eveline. Had you noticed?'

'I don't find it too bad to open. I'll be going in later. Do you want me to let you know if it catches again?' Eveline spoke brightly to him.

'Yes, Miss Eveline. Doors are fickle. This one'll be a bit more difficult to open from the inside. You keep an eye out.'

Stanton had not always been as approachable as this. He had been taciturn when Eveline had first arrived six weeks ago. Mrs. Dawson told her that Yorkshire men could be difficult to get to know.

'But, he'll have to get used to you, Miss Eveline, because you're all we've got in this house. Not like it were at Compton Agnes.'

'Is it very big?' Eveline had asked.

'There's two houses, that's what. One's all grand and full of panelling and pictures and the older, much older house, is used like a great barn. There were twenty of us, but Sir Arnold cut to ten and her Ladyship isn't pleased with him.'

'Are there grandchildren?' said Eveline, thinking of the village children back home.

'There's just the one girl, aged three now, but not likely to be another, if her Ladyship is to be believed. The Nursemaid'll soon be replaced by a Governess, I don't doubt.' Dawson turned as she spoke, determined to get on, convinced she'd said enough. Gossip is like fine wine, she'd learned. It's not good to take too much at once.

The road across the Wolds was unrelentingly long and bleak. If Bridlington had once been a Roman outpost and port, then it was at an undisputed long distance, taking its now differently paved way to Stamford Bridge. With Cartaret at the reins, the road was much more a matter of clear geography than military intent. Over and up went the contours and up and over went the horses. As they journeyed on to Driffield, Arnold looked about with his hunter's eye for birds.

'This is just the time of year for stone curlews, James. You know the three I have in the cabinet? John Wymondham put them in a scene of bracken and it's all wrong. I need a fourth and then I'll get him to adjust things. I'll pay him well. I want it right.'

James Cartaret, Mayor of Bridlington, smiled indulgently as he turned to Arnold from his forward gaze on the horses' backs.

'When we arrive at Driffield, I'm staying over and returning to Bridlington. I've found a good man to take you on in this carriage, Sir Arnold.'

'What's the hurry to be back for God's sake? This is the best April for travel I've known in a decade. I'd soon have taken the train.' said Arnold and a scowl crossed his face.

'It's the Census, Sir Arnold. I need to be back in Bridlington for the day of the return.' James Cartaret looked forward again as he spoke. Arnold could imagine his face as he considered the horses and other goods and chattels. The Census was all about place and status.

'Oh, so it is. Thursday, isn't it? Oh, well, my wife will be adding her name and my daughter's and probably not for the last time. I'm often at my Club.'

Arnold spent many months away from home. In London he negotiated the purchases of rare birds from abroad for his aviaries at Compton Agnes. House parties in the Shooting Season kept him away for almost a month, all over the country. It was then that he shot or trapped the moorland and hilltop birds of England and Scotland for his stuffed bird collection housed in Compton Agnes's Long Gallery. No-one in the Hall understood his fascination or liked what he did, particularly his mother. He would be at her house for the Census return, caught like a bird in the light, in an unwelcome place. He coughed.

'This weather's holding up for the young birds.'

'Don't just stand there, Miss Eveline. We've got work to do!' Mrs. Dawson spoke loudly and sharply to her as she went down the stairs beside the linen room, where the door stood open showing her standing with an armful of towels.

'I'm coming,' Eveline replied.

It was Wednesday and all the earlier days of the week had been spent dusting and polishing. The bright days of this April had poured a warming sunshine into the grand rooms and Dawson saw dust as a bird might the tip of a grub in the lawn.

'He's such a fussy man, I know,' Dawson had said. 'He's always down in his London Club and those places gleam with leather and wood, I'm told. That sun shows up the dust.'

Eveline wanted to be out of doors then. 'That sun' was a call to the freshness of a warmed morning on the top fields at Cold Higham or on her walk to the Minster Green to find the towers laced from the East with a centuries' old shimmer.

The man hired by Cartaret heard Arnold coughing in that cold early morning air of the Wolds. He was evidently on the lookout for birds, flying high and over into the brightening fields. Then, it was under Walmgate Bar. Sir Arnold Benyon looked curiously at the shadows. 2pm and a good time to be at mother's this sunny afternoon. Cartaret had provided an excellent man from Driffield. He had said little, just as he should, leaving the Baronet, his passenger, to his own thoughts.

They drove along Walmgate into Fossegate and over Ouse Bridge. The rounded arches of Micklegate Bar reared up over Arnold before he could clear his thoughts of the city around him.

London's bustling streets and York's hemmed-in pavements were hated haunts. Mother's house was just up the Mount and on the right.

Mrs. Dawson and Stanton were at the steps of Mount House as the carriage arrived. Stanton took the horses round to the rear and Sir Arnold entered his mother's modern town house.

Eveline came into the Drawing Room responding to the bell which rang at 4pm.

'We'd like tea, Evie,' said the mistress of the house.

She was seated opposite a man whose bulky figure filled the chair in which he sat. His mother's pale-blue afternoon dress flounced with its ribbons and layers to the carpeted floor. Eveline saw that the gentleman's leather shoes, ostentatiously placed well forward towards his mother, were dark brown and fiercely polished.

When Eveline returned with the tea service, the shoes and their owner were placed in front of the window. Sir Arnold had his back to her as she set the tea things on the table. He had gaiters and a dark brown suit which flared at the back. He had his hands in the trouser pockets and did not turn while she was in the room nor at his mother's, 'Thank you, Evie.'

At evening dinner Sir Arnold was more talkative. Dawson had shown him to his room. He had changed and he looked more at ease in a dinner jacket and silk scarf. Mrs. Dawson and Eveline served the meal as a deft partnership and Sir Arnold looked on, with glances toward his mother.

'This seems to be working well for you, mother,' he said.

'Yes, Arnold,' was her reply.

Mrs. Dawson was so relieved after clearing the meal that she told Eveline to take the rest of the evening off. Eveline changed and stayed in her room to write a letter to her parents and younger brothers.

'........Sir Arnold has arrived and the meal has gone well. We were all so worried about it.

Cook said turbot was difficult, but she was probably exaggerating to make us admire her. There were four different sauces for the fish and vegetables.

I'm going to visit the Minster in the next fortnight. I've been invited by the Lady's maid from the house opposite ours. We met in Blossom Street last week. She's called May and she's only a bit older than me. It'll be nice to have company. I'll post this tomorrow when Sir Arnold is gone......'

Eveline put the letter to one side and made the decision to settle down. The faintly-heard household noises from below had stopped a little while before. Mrs. Dawson would be in her downstairs rooms. Lady Benyon would have retired and the visitor might be smoking on the terrace. She decided to fetch a towel for her basin wash and went down the stairs to the turn.

It was then that she heard steps on the stairs below her. Eveline was quick on her feet and went into the linen room, intending to close the door behind her. It was late to be there and, if the door jammed as it had been doing, she couldn't call to anyone. So, as she turned, Eveline gently made sure that it didn't catch as she shut out the faint light on the stairs. Just as she did so, she felt the door firmly coming open towards her. Cold air and cold shadow to recall for many years to come pushed into the room where she was so discreetly placed.

Sir Arnold Benyon took advantage of the unexpected encounter. He was a large man, used to being quick and uncompromising and Eveline hated what he did. He left her shivering and shocked and she sat down on the floor of the room feeling like a rabbit might to find its burrow blocked and home inaccessible at the very moment of quivering and turning. Eveline pulled her skirt and petticoat back into place and stood up to go back to her room. She saw herself pulling the unresisting linen room door to and she saw herself in the mirror of her room, crying quietly.

The next morning, Sir Arthur had briefly breakfasted and his carriage and man had taken him back to Bridlington.

Mrs. Dawson came into the kitchen as Lady Benyon's later breakfast was almost ready to go up.

'We have to put our names on the Census form for today. It's everyone who's been in the house overnight.' Mrs. Dawson looked at her closely. 'Eveline, add yours. You haven't slept well, have you?'

'Not too well, Mrs. Dawson,' replied Eveline, looking down at the form. She had to write her name under 'Arthur Benyon, Baronet', and, with Mrs. Dawson watching, that she did, 'Eveline Maynard, Housemaid'.

After breakfast, Eveline was handed a letter from home:

'.....It does seem odd not to have your name ready for the Census Return this Thursday, but you are in a much grander place now.....'

Eveline found May the following week to cancel the visit to the Minster. Only two weeks later she gave in her notice at The Mount. There was to be a child from those moments in the linen room. It was not a person recorded on that Census day, but the father's name is clearly written there.

# The Tree House

'I don't want to know you, stuck up there!' Samantha shouted to her brother, Angus. 'Get down and come for a fight!'

She walked off up the long garden to the house and scuffed her feet on the best part of the lawn reserved for guests.

'He hogs the whole place,' she muttered.

Seeing Samantha at a distance, Angus relaxed in his edifice.

It was at a height of fifteen feet in a large Leylandii that the house was wedged as cosily as a bird box in a pear tree. Angus's father had planned it all with a local carpenter who had made several in the area before.

Tree homes have to be as bespoke as the tree, original to its grand design. Get the base up to its widest girth and take it from there. Hang, jam, enclose the wooden walls through the lifted branches angled just where you wish they were not, but dad had said no cutting allowed. Angus remembered so clearly that no harm was to come to the tree because the children wanted a hideout there.

'I'll make it up to her later,' thought Angus as he sat down in his corner.

Angus was nine at the beginning of it all, and the tree house was his joy. He watched very carefully as his father checked out the carpenter who came to build it. His name was Jack.

'Can I call you Steeplejack?' asked Angus straightaway.

''Course you can,' he replied smartly, 'but I don't go higher than this if I can help it.'

'I want to go high up,' said Angus, 'and I'd like to be higher if I could.'

'It's just at the right height for you,' said Jack, looking at this lanky lad. 'How old are you?'

'I'm nine,' said Angus. 'Dad said I'd have to wait until now for good balance. The TV programmes show boys in Africa getting up trees all the time, though. I could have done it younger.'

Angus had a straight gaze for a nine year old. Jack was quite taken with his forward manner.

'The point about this tree house is that it's as wide as it's high, if you see,' said Jack, using his hands to show Angus. 'On a wide platform, you've got more space instead of being squashed higher up the tree.'

Angus got it. 'A floor up a tree sounds funny, doesn't it? There's nothing underneath.'

'Oh, you won't fall,' said Jack. 'You're far too sensible for that.'

It wasn't too many months later that Angus wished he had fallen flat on his face. Samantha, his younger sister, had not really taken to the house at all. She was an adventurous seven year old, but she was convinced that the whole project was not an adventure to her liking.

Angus was sure she'd come round and make a den up there with him, but she never did. He watched her meander round in the garden as she returned to the house. She was probably bothered about dad, now posted away to the Gulf as a Squadron Leader. She whined when she was younger, but now she fretted by aiming at him.

'You'll never be like daddy,' she scorned him one day as a determined eight year old to his ten years. 'Daddy goes all the way up to the top and over the clouds. You'll never get that far, Angus. I know you won't.'

'I don't want to do exactly what daddy does,' Angus couldn't help yelling in reply.

'Well, you should, 'cause I can't, can I?' Sammy's pitched voice squealed out her anger at being a girl and different. She was in despair at being ordinary, unnoticed, expected, committed to a well-trodden path. The Sammy in her welled up like poisoned water.

'You'll get as dusty as the floor of the tree house,' she said to him as he came in the garden door one day. 'And you smell of it all over now, Angus. You're like the leaves on your silly tree. They fall off.'

Angus had to admit to the truth of her taunt and dusted himself down.

'It's only pine needles dropping,' he said. 'It's an evergreen tree. They're the biggest and best, Sammy.'

'Well, it's not the best tree to me,' said Sammy and moved forward to slap Angus on his arm. 'It's not going to last for ever. It will come down! It will come down!' she cried as she ran off.

It wasn't just the taunts or her youthful enthusiasms barbed at him, it was also the tricks that Sammy played on him.

About a year after the tree house was built, Sammy began on a seige for a few days. It was school Summer holidays and Angus had settled into a different routine with careful ease as he usually did, mindful of Sammy's moods. Sammy removed the tree house ladder and hid it. How she did it the first time it was difficult to see.

The ladder was of a specially designed lightweight metal, but it was long, and unwieldy in bad weather. Sammy took it away, tiptoeing to the long grass at the upper end of their garden. She laid it down flat, tidied the area with her toes and then whistled and hummed all the way back to the house, avoiding mum and the visitor as was the expectation.

Mum came along in a bother. The friend having coffee with her up at the house was left alone.

'Angus, I can see it's gone, but I can't see where it is and I can't find Sammy,' she called up to Angus anxiously. 'Don't you dare come down on your own. You know you mustn't do that, dad said.'

'I won't Mum, but how did she do it? It's a heavy ladder.'

'It's her vicious determination if you ask me. It isn't the fairies!' said his mother as she went off to explain to her guest. 'I'll just see to Celia, then I'll get back to you, Angus.'

It was an hour before mum was ready and relieved of her entertaining. She knew she had no need to worry about Angus immediately. He was self-assured, resourceful and not an anxious child. He always calmed her down. In one way, it was a simple test of endurance, not of loneliness, but of his sister's caprices.

'Found it, Angus!' she finally yelled at him down from the long grass. 'I'll find Sammy later,' she also called, but less loudly.

131

As his mother came along to lift the ladder to the platform step, Angus looked down on the action from above. His mother had the ladder over her shoulder as she walked, as if she had two long spears ready to throw at an enemy. It wasn't fun for mum to be left alone with dad flying, however experienced he was.

'Wish I could help you,' he called across to her.

'Oh, I can manage all right.' she said with a serious smile. 'It's just managing Sammy'.

She arrived at the base, tipped the ladder forward onto the ground prongs and eased the rest over to meet Angus's hands.

'Don't come down,' she said. 'I'll come up.'

She placed a polished high-heeled shoe on the bottom rung and carefully positioned one after another to mount the other rungs. Angus could not see her feet, only a head of hair advancing. Mum hadn't been up much at all since the early days last year.

'That's nice, Mum,' he said as he guided her in. It did seem like a cockpit with a co-pilot trained alongside you. Mum didn't even look breathless, but ready for more, as if they were off on a long flight.

'There's the plank seat, Mum, sit down,' he said and went to move off a few books for her. He went down on one knee as he did so, almost before he got to the bench.

'You'll get splinters like that, Angus,' laughed his mother, then saw his face. 'What's wrong?'

'Oh, nothing. My knee gets stiff sometimes. I've been hunched up waiting, I suppose.'

'Maybe,' said his mother. 'Let's pull up that trouser leg and have a look.'

Angus sat on the bench and quickly pulled up his jeans to the knee.

'It's a bit swollen, don't you think?' said Mum and put her hands round his other knee for comparison through the fabric. 'What do you think?' she asked.

'It's just achey, Mum. It'll be all right when I get more exercise back at school.'

His mother left to climb gingerly down and Angus watched the retreating scene of bobbing hair and bent shoulders of a working woman, working alone.

Sammy didn't get a punishment this time because Mum was more concerned about Angus, but she did say something.

'I can't see you've a reason for doing that, Sammy. You wouldn't like to be left alone up in the tree house.'

'I wouldn't go up there, mummy, not on my own like he does. I'd ask my friends. Angus never does,' Sammy pertly replied.

'That's the trouble now,' said her mother. 'It's Boarding School because of your father's posting and all his friends are there.'

That same month, and hiding it in long grass left uncut, Sammy chose to use a trip wire. Out shopping, she wangled her way into a fishing tackle shop to see the goldfish and bought a reel of nylon fishing wire.

That sunny day, Angus was out and about quite early. The sun caught a morning dew spotting only the taller grass at the sides of the garden, but the wire was hidden in the drier middle. He went down with a trip, a hop and skip and you only had to be there to see his face register fear of the sort an eleven year old schoolboy should not know. He didn't call to Sammy. He didn't call at all. He sat up, holding his leg tightly and squeezing it as hard as he could, keeping the cries of pain at bay. In a few minutes he was flat on the grass, lying down to recover and giving Sammy great satisfaction as she came up to him.

'Sunbathing early, Angus?' she teased and saw his face trying to find a smile for her silly prank.

Angus coughed. 'Nice one, Sammy, but get Mum can you? I think I've winded myself like I do in gym lessons.'

Sammy went off to the kitchen to find Mum, but walked backwards most of the way saying, then shouting, 'You're out of practice. Mr. Baxter will take you out of the team. You won't make it to the second team even.'

Angus hardly heard her taunts. He was as still as he could be on the sunny ground, warmed by a pain he knew he shouldn't have and wondering how it had got so deep into his body.

'I can get up, Mum,' he called when he saw her coming. She was holding Sammy fiercely by her right arm and she brought his sister right up to him to apologise.

'What do you say, you little horror?' demanded Mum, completely beside herself with dismay. This should never have happened. Why Angus wasn't up on his feet was her dominating thought and she jerked her daughter for every one of the same unclear sort in her puzzled mind.

'I didn't think you'd fall right over, Angus. Sorry,' said Sammy, looking up at her mother instead of down at Angus.

'Well, he shouldn't have done, don't you see?' cried out mother, letting Sammy go and kneeling on the grass beside Angus.

'It's that knee again, isn't it?' she said sternly.

'More like my whole leg, Mum,' said Angus, and fainted just where he lay.

When he came round, Sammy was coming over the grass with a glass of water, walking very quickly. Mum was on her 'phone.

'Get rid of that wire, Sammy. I'll have the water. Dr. Thompson's Practice? I'd like to make an appointment for my son, Angus Donnington.' She spoke securely, as she always did, then lifted Angus up for his drink and a hug.

'We'll get you looked at. I'll ring dad tonight.'

It wasn't long before Angus was with a specialist in Rheumatology. Mother rang father abroad and made a good case for a consultation. Far away, father felt perplexed and uneasy. He was in a very hot climate and rheumatism seemed to mean dampness and wet winds. At another level, Squadron Leader Donnington knew all about the scourge of TB in a not too distant past. It came and it took lives. He rang his wife back.

'How long has Angus felt stiff, Elaine?' he asked her.

'Difficult to say, Robert. He's been such a built up sort of character and he doesn't say much. When he did, I was very surprised, to tell you the truth. Sammy's been ragging him a lot, but that's nothing new,' replied Elaine. She didn't want Robert to worry unduly.

'Keep her off his back, Elaine,' he said. 'Keep me informed of progress.'

He got the news sooner than they both had anticipated. The Consultant concluded that Angus had Leukaemia and it was quite advanced. He had to start treatment.

'Can't believe it, Elaine,' said Robert very agitatedly over the 'phone. 'I'm getting some time off and I'll be home in a week.'

'Thank God,' said Elaine.

Sammy came to see Angus in Hospital. He was set up with a drip and wires and she began to look very afraid.

'I'm glad you can talk back to me, Angus. You look as if you're part of the bed.'

'Sammy, don't say that,' said her mother. 'He'll soon be off it after this treatment, and that won't be long.'

She looked anxiously at her son, wearing a thin smile of comfort and expectation.

Then she saw the floor of the tree house and the long seat placed on one side. Was Angus always lying down up there, she suddenly thought. She looked at Sammy, sitting on the edge of her chair. Sammy was fidgeting. Angus was so still.

The next week, Angus was brought home and began to walk about the house. He'd gone quite thin, but they were told that would happen. He would build up and could go back to school. His father was taken aback.

'Now I'm home, we'll see you a great deal more energetic first, Angus.'

'Well dad. I'd like to get back to my friends. I'll get my energy back when I see them. We'll get a ball out, then I'll feel better.'

'We could set you up here, Angus. Let's get you up at the treehouse,' said his father.

'He's grown out of it now, dad. There'll be moss all over the floor,' said Sammy.

'Have you been up?' asked Angus. 'When did you go? I've got some things I want from there.'

His father looked awkward at this. He wasn't at all happy with secret places, only lookouts, towers, observation posts. These were what height was about.

'We'll pick them up another day, Angus. The weather's all right, even for rotting tree houses,' he said and looked smartly at Sammy who was going to sit on his lap. 'I've come from a drier place.'

'What's it like over there, dad?' asked Angus. He reached out with his leg to stretch it better.

'Oh, we don't get to see that much,' said Squadron Leader Donnington, putting an arm around Sammy. 'It's all hot air really. It's a big camp and I'm busy all right, but I'm glad to be home for a month to see you get better.'

'I'll be all right, dad. The nurses told me that the younger ones don't have much of a chance with this, but I'm strong. It'll be good to get back to school,' said Angus.

Robert Donnington looked at them both. 'Lucky you, together at school because I'm out in the Gulf. That's what it's for, to keep you together.'

'I don't see much of Angus, dad,' said Sammy. 'We're not in the same year now that Angus is coming up to thirteen. None of the girls see much of their brothers.' She managed to look pleased.

'Well, you're seeing him now Sammy, so keep looking,' laughed her father.

Over the next few weeks, Angus adjusted to his new routine. Care with hygiene, watching for sneezes, keeping warm on a cool summer's day and nowhere too taxing to walk or to climb. He missed the tree house even though he had not been in it for some months. The ladder had been laid down underneath it and was nearly invisible in the grass. Angus sat in the conservatory a lot, plugged in, as his mother often said, meaning both his gadgets and his medical equipment.

With the school staff made aware of some of the possible outcomes, Angus and Sammy went back to School in September. Angus was to have fortnightly checks at the London Hospital to which he had been referred and the routine of the term calmed everyone's nerves as Angus went his own way again, keeping his friends amused and his teachers considerate. It was a different atmosphere for everyone as Angus was made way for, given preference on the Games field or off it and loaned a friend to be there with him in those Library times off games.

Christmas came and went with all the tensions of a Forces life. Robert couldn't get home, Elaine seemed to be surrounded by care but was careful herself not to care too much. The presents seemed more than adequate. The New Year visit to the Consultant came.

'He'll need calipers and crutches, Mrs. Donnington. We want to keep him as active as possible. A sure-fire boy like your son ought to play hard and rest hard. It's best for his condition at the moment.'

Elaine knew Robert would be pleased. It was just the making it happen at school all day and in the evenings. She called in on the Housemaster.

'He'll want to do everything as the weather warms up a bit, but there's got to be the resting as well. The specialist was insistent. Angus's father will ring every evening, although his timings might be a bit out, owing to distance, but he wants to do it instead of me. I'll come at weekends.'

As the concerned man nodded to her, Elaine saw the long evenings lightening under his watchful gaze. She would be the midnight watcher, with all too seeing eyes which wouldn't close.

Easter was early in Angus's fourteenth year. Elaine drove to his school a week before the end of term at Angus's request. The hedgerows of Surrey seemed disfigured with a brown-ness of the same colour as the soil that fixed them in place, but the return journey was lighter. Elaine could see Angus's pinched face in her front mirror. He liked the movement of the car which lightened his limbs.

'Dad's all right, then, Mum. It's been a long stint for him. We've had such good chats on the 'phone.'

Robert flew back immediately for Angus's Hospital admittance the next day.

It was all over. Angus died that first Tuesday afternoon in the hospital bed at Great Ormond Street.

Father and mother drove over to the School to collect Sammy. All the staff who had taught Angus were despondent for them. There was no escape from grief. Sullen, silent Sammy in the back of the car was a cheerless and resigned twelve year old.

Back at home, Robert went off with Sammy to see his mother, a journey of only twenty miles. Granny needed to see someone after being at a respectful distance for so long.

It was three in the afternoon that Celia came round to the Donnington's house as she'd arranged. She didn't want to keep away, she had said, as silences can be too prolonged.

'Come in, Celia. You are a dear,' said Elaine and led the way into the conservatory which seemed to ache with empty space.

'I've set the tea cups, but before we brew up, I know you won't mind if we go over to the tree house.'

'Yes, of course. I'd like to,' said Celia, moving off at the same pace as her hostess to cross the unkempt lawn and help pick up the ladder from beneath the tree.

In the afternoon light, the two ladies looked up and saw an early Spring glow take the dark leaves to task. Elaine hadn't remembered that the tree had been lopped of its top branches only a year ago. The trunk stopped about fifteen feet above the flat roof of the wooden structure where the lower long and broad branches bore up the house as was intended by Jack its maker. The higher branches grew spikily upwards at about a half right angle beyond the shortened trunk to make a deep cut heart shape in dark green twigs above.

'Let's get this up,' said Elaine quickly to Celia and the two ladies grappled clumsily with the light ladder to raise it to the platform. Elaine set out on the rungs very firmly.

'I should have done this more often. I'm out of practice.'

Celia followed once Elaine had climbed in. She lifted her head on entry to find Elaine sitting on a side bench. She went to sit just beside her to look around.

This pine, custom-built tree house was a box. From a very strong and more than substantial floor, useful for any number of pirate antics, the vertical wall planks rose like blinds taking out the light. There were two glazed windows on each side of the long bench wall and opposite was a cork noticeboard, firmly part of its build. All the originality lay in its outside placing in the branches. Within the tree house was plain, resin-smelling gloom and emptiness.

Celia spoke before she thought. 'What did he do up here?'

'Angus loved it before he was really ill,' replied Elaine. 'He must have done a lot of wishful thinking, mustn't he? He won't like mine now, Celia.'

Elaine stared at the plain floor.

'I wish it had been Sammy,' she said as her hands clutched the bench of the tree house. She shook off the arm which the astonished Celia had moved to put round her.

'It ought to have been Sammy.'

# Housemaid

Ellie skipped along the broken Hoxton kerbs, up, down, up, down, just as she'd once played with William, her older brother. 'Her Billy', they called him. Ellie was pulled right down when Billy's identity cards were sent back from France a few years before. There was a clear sniper's bullet hole made right through the paper to his chest when he was eighteen years old.

'She'll never learn, our Ellie,' her much older sister, Connie, used to say. 'Always jumping up and down, ready for the next adventure. They don't come along like 'buses, Ellie.'

It was a jumping journey to the 'bus stop and on to almost the far end of the never ending road, that Ellie was aiming for. She'd got her first job.

'What job?' shouted Gladys, the eldest of the growing cousins in her older sister's house.

'I've just been to tell your Mum,' said Ellie, coming round into the sitting room. 'It's right down Kingsland Road. Bit more than a tuppenny 'bus ride, but I'm living in for the money, too.'

'Oh, we'll miss you coming round after school,' said Gladys. Her black eyes twinkled. 'But it's a swank job isn't it?' She was pert for six years old.

'Housemaid? Yes, it's good and I'll be earning and learning. You stick at school better than I did Gladys or yer mum'll want to know why.'

Ellie's eyes met her older sister's as she turned to leave. Connie stood, arms akimbo, in the doorway smiling.

'If Mum could only see you now,' she said.

'I'm going to make a good go at this job, Connie, so she'll know. She'll be looking out for me, and there's John. I might have some money for him.' Ellie spoke fervently to Connie, her sister, her saviour. Younger brother John was struggling at school and more often than not didn't attend. A fourteen year old school leaver, Ellie felt the responsibility keenly. 'We don't know whether he'll shape up, do we?'

'No, we don't,' said Connie, 'but get on your way. Shall we see you tomorrow?'

'I'll be along after school.' Ellie jumped through the door as she spoke, intending to jump a lot more on the way home.

They were grey streets round about, but they were wide for the traffic. Carts, horses, trams, 'buses and a few cars made a haphazard journey along the high road, a route of respectability and commerce. Home was in Hoxton, a mile on, and a viciously overcrowded place. Washing hung from nearly every window on the tenement blocks. Looking up from the narrow road she had turned into, Ellie saw the outline of her home. Blackened with soot, the bricks were pock-marked and helplessly sick. The family's four rented rooms were two floors up spiral, rancid stairs too often gaining from the contents of the slop pails. They were mopped off rarely by arms which almost always had a baby or two in them.

Ellie could not know that these buildings were once well-appointed housing for the well-heeled crowds leaving London's stench a century earlier. What could she know of history? You can look over your own shoulder to a carving or a cornice and it will speak to you either that day or another day, but not over the heads of a jostling family and step-family, each taking a daily enlarging space in the same small compass.

Ellie did know how much Connie's married life enlarged her own. There were twelve years between them in age and Connie had a young family growing up in a house with a back yard. It was a heaven-sent opportunity to watch a mother at work as she could not watch her own. Connie relied on Ellie to give her a break in mid-afternoon and Ellie watched the Wednesday's baking, the potato peelings for the tin bin and the pots, pans and performance of a true house-wife, much before suburban houses demanded one. Servants, young and biddable, like Ellie, were plentiful.

When the day came for Ellie to move over to Mr. Clipstein's house, she had everything ready. It wasn't much. She wore her coat and straw hat and had a couple of dresses packed. Connie had bought her a new hairbrush for her straight, black, thick hair. Her few pairs of long drawers and what had to be fastidious for a girl were washed at night in the scullery sink at home so she'd do the same in the job. Ellie's shoes were decent and she took wadding and blacking to keep them that way.

It was more than a tuppenny 'bus ride, but not much more. The journey was along a straight Roman road. Ellie had known it all her life, crossing it often at Dalston Junction like millions on the move before her, but this time it led North and higher. That high ground was prized by the Jewish businessmen who'd moved into the grand new houses there over a decade ago. Ellie was headed for Fairholt Road, Stoke Newington.

'Get a move on there,' said the 'bus conductor to Ellie, who had to stoop below the wooden step of the 'bus to pick up her bag. It had driven in so quickly and tightly to the kerb where she was nervously waiting. It didn't seem to want to delay a second.

'So, you're getting off just before Stamford Hill? Ninepence.'

Ellie found the pence, just as she gave a wave to Connie. It was a prize price. She had an orange oblong ticket all punched and neat. She'd never been given that colour before. She wouldn't scuff it like the ones she'd picked up off the floor for her collection on shorter 'bus journeys. Ellie felt there must be fields when she arrived, even though the journey was so predictably straight, hemmed in by an ever changing array of shops and busy with crowds at junctions waiting on traffic lights. The address seemed so open in itself.

'Look at the 'o's', she thought, seeing them evenly spaced in the lines of the address on the postcard. She'd been good at handwriting at school and the letter 'o' was perfected, joined at the top to embroider itself along a page in neat, wholesome stitches. She had all good thoughts between her nervousness and the adjective was a lovely word to write, joining open 'o's of wonder along the threads of 'good'.

'Your stop, missie,' came the shout and Ellie was on the pavement of a new town, still named London.

The 'bus clung to the pavement as Ellie clutched her bag to step off. Every item in the street seemed spaced out as she stood there. The 'bus drew away behind her and, much like any newcomer left standing in a centuries-old highway, Ellie was a witness to spaces as never before in her life. The pavements here were wide, and at decent architectural intervals were high villas, trees and gates. Gate posts like sentinels, more imposing than anything she had ever seen, marched on into the middle distance where the 'bus now lurched on its way.

'Why aren't there no shops? Who really lives here?' Ellie spoke out loud, because there was no-one to hear her. She sensed a no-man's land of uncertain crossing as she set off to find her destination.

Ellie knew it was on the same side as the 'bus had dropped her because she had been told that special detail. All she had to do was find the turning, Fairholt Road, and be safe.

It was such a quiet road. Sound was sucked back to the High Road, leaving a vacuum of inertia. She met a street cleaner with his metal barrow and long broom as she cautiously paced towards him looking for the house numbers.

'How far down is number 104?' she asked him.

'Not far, Missie. What you doing round 'ere then?' He leaned on his broom to ask.

'I'm going to be housemaid,' said Ellie briefly.

'It's nice round 'ere, Missie, when you get used to it,' said the stocky man. 'You'll find it quiet though. These people keep themselves to themselves, an' no mistake.'

He spoke kindly. Ellie looked nervous enough.

Ellie walked off brightly. She didn't altogether understand what he meant, but he'd made things easier. She passed two gleaming cars before she reached her destination.

At 104 it was easy, too. No-one made her feel nervous.

Mrs. Barnes opened the side door when Ellie rang and was friendly straight away.

'You look good, Ellie Sharpe. How do you do? I'm Mrs. Barnes. You're Miss Sharpe when I speak to you and Ellie to the family when they get to know you.'

Mrs. Barnes led her downstairs to her back room bedroom.

From then on it was 'do this' and 'do that' that reminded Ellie of school. Housework was as punctual as lessons and times in between for cleaning the silver just like finishing off rows of sums for Miss Newsome, her teacher, or like the homework she used to get as extra. There was no writing though, thought Ellie, only doing. She didn't mind.

'Friday lunchtime to Sunday morning breakfast is time off for you and me,' Mrs. Barnes had carefully said and she'd pointed out the cutlery and dinner service which Ellie mustn't touch.

Ellie wasn't a Churchgoer, but she knew about Jews. There were plenty of Synagogues around Dalston and no worries bustling around with the wives all shopping frantically on a Friday.

Mrs. Barnes told her about Passover pastry, which seemed a bit of a mystery to Ellie. She'd grown up with soft dumplings in stew and eel pie if she could get it. In the smart cupboards the packets and biscuits looked dry and tasteless.

'When Mrs. Clipstein buys the fresh food on Fridays it always looks better,' said Mrs. Barnes. 'It's all part of their religion, you see.'

Mrs. Barnes genially simplified many things, but Ellie being quick and intelligent, got to the point at once.

'I know Saturday's the Sabbath. It's like our Sunday, only different. They don't do no work,' said Ellie clearly.

'We've got work to do, Ellie. Get a move on!' said Mrs. Barnes, shooing her away.

Ellie went off to the front parlour which joined to a small anteroom next to the spacious hall. In that room was a complex piece of furniture which Mrs. Barnes had said was the 'Shiff-on-Ear'. Musical sounding as it was, its only tune for Ellie was the playback of her reflection. Ellie polished this high-backed mahogany cupboard with its elegant fluted bars and carved edges looking at herself with honesty. The

145

white apron on the black uniform stood out as clearly as the round child's face above. She wanted to pinch herself every time she looked. How did she get this job in a wide house, set apart from her life so far down the 'bus route it could have been Fairyland?

As the months went by, Ellie found the job very satisfying. Mrs. Barnes had a good job, too. Jewish employers took their Gentile employees' needs seriously. They needed them in this politely chic, well-proportioned part of London, their enclave of quiet resilience and true conformity.

Walking back to the 'bus stop and crossing to the other side of the road became commonplace, but not her impression of grandeur as she entered the High Road. It was the one place she knew where porportion mattered. Every house, with just a few people in it, rose up around her. Her real longing for space began here.

'Ellie, what a nice cup of tea you always make,' said Mr. Clipstein one late afternoon.

'Thank you, sir,' bobbed Ellie and glowed with pride.

Learning how to make tea properly had taken quite a few weeks under Mrs. Barnes' instruction.

The boiling kettle bubbled badly and burnt her fingers at first, but once she got the hang of the sound of the water at the right temperature to pour on to the tea leaves, she could make it properly every time.

It was the sound of bubbling water which led Ellie to a final adventure, one which no-one could have foreseen and no-one wanted.

'Ellie!' called Mrs. Barnes, 'run Mrs. Clipstein a bath before you go off. She wants one a bit earlier than usual.'

Ellie was packing her small bag for her two nights away. She put it down on her bed and went quickly to the back stairs. It was three flights to the bedroom floor and she went forward to the bathroom suite.

When she turned on the boiler tap, no hot water came through, but just a few short bubbles. Ellie took a box of matches from the cupboard to relight the pilot at the side of the gas boiler over the bath.

It was then the boom reached her ears and the flare of the gas flame hit her retreating face. It was just like a bomb in her ear. The quick jet of flame, the smell of two types of burning; hair and the choked jet. The sound was louder than the machine guns which her brother had braved before the lone sniper spotted him and so she covered her ears and screamed. She screamed with the fear of the screams she had lain awake and heard when her mother died in childbirth having John. She had been just as alone as Ellie was in a small, damp room. Into this deafening noise of Ellie's fears came Mr. and Mrs. Clipstein.

Ellie had singed eyebrows and had a reddened face, but that little pent up pocket of gas had done no real damage to her or to the room. She sat outside on the rug in the upper hall, sobbing very noisily. All the peace of her life in this house had been boomed away. No war was safe, perhaps no peace was safe.

'You'll be all right, Ellie, there, there,' said Mr. and Mrs. Clipstein and they meant it and knew it.

Mrs. Barnes was amazed. 'Just a little flame to make a bang like that?' she cried.

'We'll get it seen to, but Ellie's all right, that's the main thing. Mrs. Barnes, take the double fare and get Ellie home on the 'bus. Give Ellie the change.' said Mr. Clipstein.

He handed Mrs. Barnes two half-crowns.

'I won't come back, I won't come back,' Ellie said through her lessening sobs. The fear that was the birthright of a Hoxton child had stalked her all the way to this well-run house and exploded in her face.

She got up to go with Mrs. Barnes to take the 'bus home.

# Strangers

Laurie sauntered up the High Street, practising a secure walk. It meant no hands in the grey trouser pocket, no shuffle as he usually did in London. He was in Oxford to chance it and practice would make his chances perfect.

He saw a bench, got out a notebook and small pencil and sat to draw a quick map. He was sitting quite near to a pedestrianised area. It was a wide road with the usual cache of shops and none of any use to him, not to Laurie Swinton.

It was just as a passer-by looked at him and decided to join him that Laurie knew he had to practise more. He looked at a loose end and that wouldn't do.

'Making the most of the sunshine?' said the man as he sat down beside Laurie amicably, not too close, but close enough to see the map Laurie had sketched. Laurie saw his thin dark blue sweater out of the corner of his eye and the near arm's woollen sleeve had come down to grip the bench with a mottled hand. It was a worn sleeve, well enough worn for this man not to be seen as a companion.

'Can't say that I am,' replied Laurie, slowly closing his notebook. 'I'm finding my bearings.'

'You're new here, then?' challenged this sweatered man whose face Laurie had not yet seen. A voice was enough of a threat to Laurie.

'I've been here a few days, showing up with what I sell,' said Laurie, piecing a line and looking askance at the busy corner with its passing nondescripts and pre-occupied young mothers.

The arm relaxed its grip on the bench to replace it on a lap. Grey trousers covered the legs beneath the hands, Laurie saw, and he was not pleased.

'I don't buy or sell any more,' said the man beside him. 'I'm happiest with a wander and a sit down. It suits me fine and especially this weather.'

The hand rose as if to pull a fair early summer afternoon in from the road itself. The man had a compass no further than the reach of an outstretched hand.

'I'll get a move on,' said Laurie as he rose and turned to look fleetingly at the bench. There sat a well-built man in a V-necked sweater and a College tie, striped blue and red, tucked neatly in.

Laurie's farewell was just this cursory glance, but he'd turned his back on a good disguise, he thought, although he knew he'd get away with a blue tie. He pulled his jacket down as he walked away. It was a dark blue linen, easily creased, long since new and looking like well-loved denim in its patina, but it would serve him well.

Laurie went along the pedestrianised street at a modestly quick pace, eyes ahead with somewhere to go written firmly on his face. At the far end, he paused beside an illustrated map of the City and took stock of himself for a final time. He really needed to improve his self-conscious walk into a convincing moderate pace. He couldn't enter a College without it.

Jane Seaman was also in the pedestrianised road, walking along with an air of confidence. This was holiday, but with the chance of study at an Oxford College. It was promotional work for her school. She had got through the ballot stage for the place, had her College and room allocated and had already met some of the other researchers, each of whom was awaiting an interview with a resident tutor, taking holiday time to be with them. As a system it was as fair as any in English education. Apply, justify, descend, enjoy and a worthwhile experience was yours at every level of College life for a short week.

Jane's briefcase held a few documents, but there was more to Oxford than Libraries, rules of entry and Reader cards, as this international community summered and shopped and bought almost as much as the tourists from London, whose cameras snapped a scene before they snapped a bargain. She entered Crawley's, a boutique she'd spotted down a side street with a Summer Sale-promoting A-board on the pavement.

'Good afternoon,' said the shop owner, busy with tissue paper at the desk.

'Hello,' said Jane. 'Can I browse?'

'Yes, of course,' came the reply. Then came the encouraging sounds of hangers being shifted along rails, with the sight of all tags being scrutinised and assessed.

'Are you looking for anything in particular?' said the shop owner, pushing tissue paper to one side and coming forward with an elegant step. Too close is an affront to relaxed shopping.

Jane turned and smiled, ready to offload a few hints about Dinner at College, a new jacket, what her husband would say and why Summer Sales were always at a good time in Oxford. She saw the shop owner sum her up immediately as a figure to dress. There would be something tailored with a hint of nonchalance, a darkish colour but not black, and with small motifs. She had everything in Jane's size.

'Our Lavina range would suit you,' said the shop owner. 'Try this rail. I don't think you spotted it round the corner. Everything's reduced.' She led Jane to an area near to the Changing Room. The rail had a range of sleeved jackets and jacket style cardigans in shades of coffee, chocolate, mint greens and creams. The subtlety tempted Jane into a purchase of a frilled jacket cardigan in dark grey, green and cream overlaid striping with buttons of each colour between the frilled front fastening. Its unusual lack of symmetry was quite satisfying and Jane would wear it over black trousers at the College Dinner that evening. It was formal, but flouncy, expensive looking but bought at an affordable price. In the sturdy card bag, the purchased item sat firmly in its taped tissue and most female shoppers would have continued their meandering with just exactly Jane's self- conscious pleasure.

Laurie and Jane each measured their different steps along the same central pedestrianised street in Oxford. Sightseers sent to relax and shop crowded the late afternoon just before 5pm. Pizza restaurants were full even to the upstairs level with the peckish who had to wait for an Institution's punctual evening meal. There really was a hum in the air, of discordant languages and laughter and an unfathomable warmth not altogether related to a summer's day. Laurie's suit felt slightly sticky with the sweat of his shirt. Jane's briefcase held in the same hand as her Boutique bag, knocked gently against her legs as she walked to her College gate.

Laurie was there before her.

He nodded to the Porter just as he was turning to pick up a key from the board behind him and stepped over the ledge of the old blackened gate from the kerbside. Laurie walked with considered purpose into the first quadrangle where an early evening sun had gathered for almost six centuries. He did not look up or around. He was not a visitor nor tourist but one of the fold, further enfolded into this softness of warmed stone and emerald green diamond cut grass. His arms moved in the confident rhythm of his body. Only his head needed to be placed more forward on his shoulders with aim, as if he knew where he was going, which he did not.

The next archway led to an open, more modern area which he had seen from an angle when sizing up his chances. He'd walked by the electronic service gate a few times yesterday morning. The tall corner block beyond was accommodation and he suspected he would be very accommodated there. His walk slowed slightly, but only very slightly as a Porter was to be seen coming up the slope from the surrounding gardens.

'Good evening,' said the man politely to Laurie who nodded distinctly in his direction as he moved off diagonally to the Students' residence. Its recently built concrete tower was a light grey in colour both inside and out. A spiral staircase went clockwise from the left. Laurie placed his feet firmly on the first step and got ready to walk up six flights.

'Good evening, Miss,' said the same Porter to his next visiting student, Jane Seaman.

'Good evening,' she replied. 'It's lovely, isn't it?'

The man stopped to talk.

'You lot in Abney always get the best week in July,' he said with a smile.

'Well, we're teachers on holiday. When do you get to take yours?'

'In snatches, Miss. There's never a dull moment here.'

He passed on with the smile of a trusted employee and Jane reached the tower doorway to squeeze through as she put it to herself. This was the second day of her week here and when she had been given her key and shown up by a Porter on day one, she noticed how cramped were the stairs, lifts and doorways for anything more than the narrowest of suitcases or flimsiest of backpacks. The rooms off opened out with a more adequate space for study and a few friends in.

Jane stood with briefcase and bag just long enough to decide on the lift for her fourth floor. It was at ground level and the grey steel door opened. It was a lift for four as long as they were not large and the steel sides were quite battered by luggage she noted as she put her briefcase down.

The lift stopped at the second floor. Jane picked up her briefcase as the door opened and moved over a little for Laurie, who looked blandly at her.

'Going up?' said Jane as Laurie entered. 'It'll be fourth or are you at the top?'

'Top,' replied Laurie and the lift ascended.

'It's seven o'clock for Dinner, isn't it?' said Jane, looking encouragingly at Laurie. His face was square-cut, clean shaven. His greying hair needed a cut, but no more than the busy husband she had left at home. She reckoned he'd change for Dinner from his day jacket and grey trousers. It was what everyone did.

'See you later,' she said as she stepped out on the fourth and left the man in the blue-grey steel lift.

Jane went straight to the small communal fourth floor kitchen to put the kettle on. It was six o'clock, so there was time for a mug of tea before the formality of the evening. A few papers to look through and a chance to try on her purchase and the evening was assured. She thought she'd make some 'phone calls to the family after the College Dinner.

Five minutes to seven and Jane was ready to go over to Hall. As she left and locked her door, she heard the other room occupant of her side of the stair well moving about. Jane had met her on the first night, when she had spoken to most of the women in the twenty strong group. She was called Abbi and was teaching at a vast school in South London. She had set her sights on a significant promotion, she'd said, and was preparing a year's programme for Governors. She was smartly dressed last night, Jane had noted, with red stripes on a shirt dress. Abbi appeared to know the way forward.

At the Hall where the twenty had a convenient side room, the Vacation Study Group stood around the central table to converse. It was not subtle conversation, but about type of school, weather, teaching skill, choice of subject and sometimes family left at home. Jane was talking to Gerald who came from somewhere south of Birmingham.

Seven o'clock came and the assembled company sat down. One chair was vacated.

'Someone forgotten to unbook their meal,' said Gerald to Jane. 'It's complicated, though, going to the Porter's Lodge and spilling the beans about going to the cinema instead. Do they have to know everything about us?'

As he spoke Abbi came hurriedly in and took her place at the table.

'I'm very sorry,' she explained. 'I forgot the time up there. My lap top takes a few minutes to turn off and I misjudged things.'

Her smile was so sincere that no-one minded. Each guest was supposed to be a gentleman on account of an honest CV and a justifiable project. The serving ladies looked relaxed. It was a fine evening. Five minutes late to Dinner with the just was no real offence. Those who saw such things noticed the cream flouncy blouse as the napkin was whisked off the plate and placed on Abbi's lap. Jane felt very fitting in the new top and chatted to Gerald as the meal went on.

Later, upstairs, after a slow walk up the staircase, Jane found the door to her room jemmied away from the jamb and she stood holding a useless key in perfect fear. She went into her room. Nothing had been taken whilst they were all at Dinner because Abbi had evidently disturbed the burglar, and he had run off.

Jane went back to the gentlemen still chatting in the Dining annexe. Abbi was seated in a low armchair sitting well back, arms raised along the velveteen sides, looking as if the day was done.

'Could I interrupt?' said Jane to everyone there. 'A burglar has been in the accommodation block and my room door has been broken into.'

'Oh, my God, my laptop!' said Abbi, beginning to hoist herself up.

'Your room door looks okay,' said Jane hurriedly, then quickly took the hint from one of the company to get to the Lodge to report.

'I'll come with you,' said Gerald.

As they walked over, Jane said little, but had the fearful realisation which she blurted out.

'I met the burglar in the lift. I thought he was one of us!'

Laurie had left quietly just as Abbi had sat down at table. He went through the Goods entrance with two young American students resident in a different block who were aiming for the local pub. Laurie had nothing to sell, not even to pay for a fizzy drink.

Jane had her briefcase and belongings taken by the Porters to another room that night. It seemed to sit at a disjointed angle on the building's second floor, mirroring the original room and parodying its insecurity. Jane was headed for a fruitless and frightening week as she relived her meeting in the lift again and again in Police interviews and ever more fitful dreams.

# 31<sup>st</sup> November

It was cold, but fresh and bright as Miss Beatrice Beast looked out at the south garden from the long high window in her Governess rooms.

'This is the day for an outing,' she yawned to Alice, who was stoking up the room's small fire and yawning herself, although it was 8am already.

'Are you sure, Miss Beast?' she said, looking round. 'It might not last. It never does when I get a day off.'

'Mark my words it will be fresh enough for a picnic,' laughed Miss Beast lightly. The sun would be a pleasing aspect for the day, especially when the day meant taking over Charlotte and Thomasina from their nurse at 10am. Her two charges were a lively five year old and a precocious seven year old. Their brother James was away at Eton. The girls missed their brother and had been restless since he went off two months ago, waving from the top of his box trunk on the chaise, 'I'll be back for Christmas. We'll have our fun then.' With their mother and father away in India on an Army posting, Captain James Jocelyn's spacious Hall home was overseen by his brother John, a Magistrate.

Beatrice looked out at the garden again.

'It's a little misty,' she said to Alice, who came to join her at the window. 'Is no-one up and about? Will Denbigh be about today?'

'He's been called away to his sister's, Miss Beast, and we're none of us sure when he'll be back, yet.' Alice decided to say more, to set another scene. 'Mrs. D's gone to join him for today and she's left broth and ham. I wonder Mrs. D didn't tell you,' she said as she looked up at Miss Beast taking in the information.

'Oh, a clear day in more ways than one,' said Beatrice. She felt her hands go cold at the wide window as she had her back to the newly lighted fire. She turned.

'Before you go, Alice, turn down the girls' beds. That will set me forward,' she said.

'Yes, Miss Beast, no trouble,' said Alice and left the room to its occupant.

Beatrice sat by the fire to warm her hands. When she had lifted her usual day dress with its black lace over her flannel petticoat that morning she had little idea that the day would begin with such unease. Beatrice had a solitary post as governess. It called for poise and self-restraint, especially in the many hours alone, but she did not like being marooned. Surely she'd see someone today, she thought.

Nora would soon bring the two girls. Beatrice took her red shawl and went through the adjoining door to her sitting room where the children did their work when not outside.

The knock came soon enough. Nora tapped, but always loudly.

'Miss Beast, ma'am, I've got them for you,' said Nora, when the door was opened.

The two girls went straight to their desks. Beatrice half closed the door on them and spoke to Nora briefly.

'Is the master here this weekend?' she said, and noted Nora's wispy hair escaping from under her cap.

'No, Miss Beast. Sir's been gone since sunrise. He took a cab to the Railway Station.'

'Where has Mr. Jocelyn gone? It's not like him not to refer to me,' said Beatrice, anxious to clarify things. 'You're off, too?' she said briefly.

'Yes,' said Nora, 'You'll be on your own a while. Luncheon and supper have been set for you. Mrs. D said she'd be back tomorrow.'

'Thank you, Nora,' replied Beatrice, but had a sudden thought.

'What is the date today?' She sounded puzzled.

'It's November 30$^{th}$. The girls are counting the days on our Calendar in the Nursery. It's nearing the time for their brother to return.' Nora smiled, happy to impart knowledge.

'I somehow thought yesterday was the 30$^{th}$,' said Beatrice, then turned with a firm nod, 'but now I know.'

In the cosy school-room, Charlotte and Thomasina were drawing on the slim notebooks they had retrieved from their desks. It was a continuation of their work yesterday. Charlotte had drawn a house and was busy landscaping with trees and sheep to dot about. She hummed very occasionally, but was otherwise quiet. Thomasina was filling in an outline of herself. She had drawn a large, fat head on very narrow shoulders yesterday. She so often copied her sister, but this was quite different.

By this time, Nora would have passed the glowering eagles on either side of the wrought iron gates. This room was the only one occupied and with a fire in the whole grand house. As the pencils scratched on the thin paper, Beatrice went to the train station in her mind.

'Where could he go for two days and nights without letting me know? Why am I solely in charge? Why am I left alone?'

'Miss Beast?' said Charlotte anxiously. 'How will I know this is right?' She pointed at her house, sketched among clouds and fields as though it floated there as firmly as in her mind.

Beatrice decided on the outing there and then.

'We'll go out to get a view of this house, then you can decide,' she said. 'Let's get your coats from the hallway.'

She opened the door on to the landing at the top of the stairs and watched as the girls held the handrail of the oak staircase. She could not hear their feet on the thick red carpet, but turned to take her tweed cape. Her hat would be ready to adjust downstairs in the hall and gloves were in her pockets.

Going down the stairs from her room she always smiled. Beatrice had been a governess in several houses over a decade and had held this post with the Jocelyn's for six months. Only in this establishment did her name seem part of the house itself. In other homes, despite her youth and good credentials, the older children she knew called her 'Beastly Beast' when they could. Here, at each turn of the grand stairs, a different oak heraldic beast greeted you as you came up, holding crests of the owner's family or of his wife's, but it was on the way down that the real charm of the creature was apparent. The monkey's tail wound jokingly up its back, the eagle's wings crossed haphazardly at the rear despite its forward upright stare and the gryphon's incongruous hooves made him the clumsiest shield-holder of them all. Miss Beast's friends, all six of them on guard.

'Are you there, Miss Beast?' called Charlotte as she and Thomasina stood by the eagle to await her.

'Here I am,' Beatrice replied. 'Tie your bonnets and I'll find your gloves.'

The three were well prepared for a crisp mid-morning walk in the sun breaking through the light mist. They would look back at the house to count windows for Charlotte's drawing and Thomasina would run through the long shadows of the three of them on the lawns, thin and neat with the slimmest stems of necks, like the narrowest of wine glasses. Beatrice kept close to the girls. No-one came into view, no dogs barked today. The air took their conversations and their cries as if it to hoard the echoes in the chill air of the wide lawn.

They turned to view the house. Its three grey brick storeys and long, evenly spaced windows shone back at them.

'I've got to draw in the top floor, Miss Beast, even though I don't know what's there,' cried Charlotte. 'I've never gone up there.'

'Well, your drawing only shows the outside,' said Beatrice.

'My footprints don't undo,' said Thomasina firmly. 'They do on green grass.'

She stood looking at the file of imprints across the frosty lawn, then played a game of light and dark with them, trying to measure feet to bonnet on a footprint each. Could she get her head shadow to twist round to the foot shadow of the footprint she had lined up for herself?

Beatrice smiled at her jerky movements, noticing none at all up at the windows of the Hall. Thomasina then promptly concluded her game and stood beside her sister to walk back.

160

Cold ham with pickle and pickled walnuts were theirs in the far kitchen next to the larder. They came in at the kitchen door and sat in their coats to eat. Beatrice had removed her cloak and laid it over the three stools on which they sat close together. It was a very satisfactory time in a large room where bustle was commonplace. Now, the trio enjoyed the echoes of pickle forks in the jar and the concluding ceremony of putting it all under the cloth, 'for Cook'.

It was after 1pm as the three walked hand in hand along the windowless corridors to the panelled hall, its staircase and its fire.

'Ooh,' said Thomasina when she saw the fire well alight. A wood boy, at least, had been up to the Hall.

'May we, Miss Beast?' said Charlotte, and at the careful nod, took her hand from Beatrice's to hold her sister's and run to the crackling fire. Beatrice took their hats and coats as they stood there to hang them in the hall cloakroom. She looked out quickly to see that the girls were sat safely by the fire. On the shelf by the windowsill was a pocket Railway timetable. She picked it up and looked at the back and front covers. There was nothing to say where Mr. Jocelyn had gone on the noisy train from York. Perhaps to Doncaster, or north and across the hills to Preston.

The girls were laughing together, so Beatrice left the cloakroom and went to the fireside to sit with them, moving aside the draped curtains close to the stairs which served to make it a room instead of a hall to pass through.

'Charlotte, Thomasina, would you like a story round the fire before we go upstairs?' said Beatrice as she drew up a high backed chair to their fender stool.

'Miss Beast, you are good to us,' said Charlotte, turning with reddened cheeks from the heat. 'That was a cold walk, wasn't it?'

'It is one by George MacDonald. You have probably heard it before, but Thomasina won't remember.'

Both girls' buttoned boots were pointing to the fire. This would be a warm story and, if Charlotte was old enough to listen well, she would transmit its excitement to her sister. Beatrice began.

'There was once a witch called Watho, who wanted to know about everything. She wanted to know why flames curled and flickered instead of going straight up the chimney,' said Beatrice, as Thomasina turned to her at the words, 'and why wood burned and why it floated, too, and she also wanted to know about people, why we always group together and tell stories, like now, and how we don't like to be alone and how much we always want to know.'

Charlotte smiled at her sister and Beatrice rushed on to keep the smile on the child's face.

'Watho found out that as she wanted to know more and more, her straight witch's back became a little more bent over with what she knew she knew, but there was still more to know.'

'It's not nice to have a bad back,' said Charlotte. 'Denbigh says so when he picks up the wheelbarrow.'

'Watho was a teacher, too, and she had two pupils, like you two are mine, except one was a boy and the other a girl.'

Charlotte straightened her apron, but it wasn't clear to Beatrice whether she felt herself the boy or the girl in the story yet.

'Watho taught the boy to be very brave because of the knowledge he would have. He learned all sorts of things for his age. He could fight with a sword, plan a battle and he had read all sorts of books on how to do those things. He could talk with Watho about everything he had learned and she encouraged him to be valiant and brave. He was always out in the daytime, practising his skills and reading by the lamp at night.'

'Miss Beast, what did the girl learn to do?' said Charlotte. She was pleased that her younger sister was warmed into silence by the heat of the fire.

'I've shortened the story, so you'll hear.' Beatrice began again.

'The girl was called Nycteris, and her lessons were in a closed up room, much smaller than this one and a bit below ground. She didn't mind,' said Beatrice hurriedly, 'because her lessons were in reading and music, so she knew quite a few stories and could sing to herself.'

'But she didn't know as much as the boy,' asked Charlotte. 'How could she?'

'In the story it seems that she knows a great deal more, because when she finally meets Watho and the boy together, he is afraid of something he knows nothing about.'

'There's lots we don't know about,' said Charlotte. 'What was it?'

Beatrice didn't mind a question and answer ending which suited her tale so well. She looked round to the north facing window opposite the fire and saw the winter afternoon light beginning to dull. 'It was just when the light in the sky was fading and the boy wanted to see the dark as he was always out in the light. Watho found him later that night crouching down on the lawn. She could see him because it was a starry night and there was a very bright moon. He was bent over like she was, not because he knew too much but because he was frightened of the moon. He didn't know what it was.'

'But the moon is always there,' said Charlotte, and Thomasina nodded firmly with her sister. 'We can see it from the Nursery.'

'He had never been shown it, so when he first saw it he was afraid. Watho couldn't get him to be brave enough to stand up to look at it, even though he'd been taught to fight with swords, so she had to bring Nycteris from her closed room to explain. She had always lived in the dark, you see.'

'What did she tell him it was?' asked Charlotte. 'Did he get up?'

'Yes, he got up in the end, but not before Nycteris explained. She came to him in the dark he couldn't understand when he was afraid of the moon he didn't know. Nycteris said, 'It is not my lamp, it is the mother of all lamps', and gradually she showed him the meaning of the moon. She couldn't show him the moon, could she, because it is too far away, but she showed him that its gentle light helps us understand the dark.'

Beatrice concluded just as Thomasina took hold of her sister's hand. She was more than ready for Nursery tea and an early night.

Nora could soon be heard coming from the corridors to the kitchen. She looked hard at the three of them so close to the fire.

As Nora and her charges went past her to their rooms, Beatrice felt again how much she needed to know when Mr. Jocelyn would return. It was darkening very quickly now. She moved along to the kitchen, feeling her way towards it down the corridors to find the setting rays of a very weak sun just lighting up the range. The warmed broth was still perfectly good. With the warmth of the fire, the broth and the release from the children, Beatrice retired for the evening to write to her brother and to read.

'It seems he left on Friday evening from York Railway Station. That could mean a long journey and to where, no-one knows. I do want to be fair, but he is being unfair to us all.' So ran a sentence or two in her letter to her brother in London.

Beatrice was still thinking about her brother as she waited in the downstairs hall for the two children and their walk to Church the next day. Nora came down with them both, looking pleased.

'Miss Beast, Charlotte wants another story this afternoon. Could you come up after their luncheon?'

Beatrice was happy enough with the arrangement and was thinking it all through as they took the path to the village. Thomasina was lively.

'No footprints on the path at all, Miss Beast,' she said.

'No, there aren't. There's no-one ahead of us today,' was Beatrice's reply.

Some looks were directed at them by villagers as there were so few in the usually full family pew.

'Some sickness has reduced us and Mr. Jocelyn has been called away,' said Beatrice in response to the anticipated query on leaving.

Their return journey was always more positive. Thomasina was still on the look- out for clues on the ground. Charlotte skipped ahead but kept in sight where the path curved.

Beatrice found Mrs. Denbigh preparing dinner after the girls had gone upstairs.

'There's more cold meat, Miss Beast. It's gammon this evening and I suppose we are to expect Mr. Jocelyn?' said Mrs. Denbigh.

'I can't be sure,' replied Beatrice. 'I've been at a loss all weekend as to why I don't know his destination so as to make a guess at his return.'

'Reasons of his own, I don't doubt, Miss Beast. We can't know everything,' said Mrs. Denbigh as she lifted the gammon into a large pan of water on the range. 'I'll be happy when things are back in place. This'll need eating up.'

Beatrice's quiet meal in her rooms was not as light-hearted as yesterday's in the kitchen. She thought up a story for the girls with each of the animals from the staircase, what footprints they would make on the ground for Thomasina and ideas for Charlotte to draw. She had a picture book of birds in the Nursery.

Nora left them together for a couple of hours. The room was a bright one just off their parents' empty bedroom. It was a peaceful wing when James was away at school. He ran around a great deal and expected his sisters to chase him.

On the window seat, full in the light, the picture book came out.

'Look at the eagle's wings,' said Charlotte.

'Now you see why our carved eagle has his wings folded, or we could not pass him on the stairs,' said Beatrice, then turned to Thomasina. 'And for you, the owl is a night bird and won't leave a footprint, will he? He swoops and flies up to a dark branch. His claws grasp it tightly.'

Charlotte looked at her sister. 'I expect his wings brush the ground sometimes,' she said, 'to make their own mark.'

When Nora arrived to conclude with Nursery tea, Beatrice had the children's drawings pinned to their bed hangings then crossed to the landing and her own rooms. She would read she thought.

An hour later, Beatrice went down to the dusk of the hall with her brother's letter. She placed it on the usual tray for collection tomorrow.

As she walked back up the stairs, she looked carefully at her creatures which were newels of uniqueness at each turn of the stairs. The eagle glared from the first step, owl followed with an uneasy stare, then the monkey's paws rested on the chiselled slab of oak. Above him the Gryphon grasped a shield of red and grey with a gold sword sinister, then it was heraldic dog and cat up at the top, nearer to the family house and home which went off to the right. Beatrice's two small rooms were ahead on the short landing and to the left was the Billiard Room, smoking room, study and bedroom for Mr. Jocelyn. He had a wing for his pursuits and she heard them so often, but where was he and what was he doing?

It was through the large Palladian window of the stairwell that Beatrice then saw the lights of a cab moving down the drive. They were eerie twin points of light, vaporising at the start of an evening fog. Beatrice walked back down the stairs, taking each turn as a thrust for her new endeavour and she took her beasts with her. The dog was at her heel, the cat around her skirts. The gryphon hopped neatly down and landed with a comfortably firm thud. She handed the monkey onto her shoulder where he nibbled gently at her lacy throat, and the two large-winged birds flew silently ahead of her to land on the tall-backed chair by the fire, together facing the doorway through which her adversary would come.

The large front door slammed, the cab removed itself and through the thick red curtain came the large, round face of John Jocelyn JP, her employer. His fat cheeks were sat on a high collar where sideburns met under the chin. His black coat and suit brought in the darker night and, as he removed his top hat to speak to her, his right hand looked poised for more than its doffing.

'Good evening, Beast,' he said, and began to walk towards the centre of the hall. The owl shifted on its carved perch.

'Good evening, sir,' began Beatrice.

'What do you have to say?' Mr. Jocelyn placed his hat on the hall table and unbuttoned his gloves to take them off. One reached the table but the other fell, to land on the edges of the rug.

Beatrice began. 'I needed to know where you were, sir, because I had the children solely in my charge these two days.'

'Oh, yes,' he said, and began to walk towards her.

Beatrice stopped him by saying, 'It is a responsibility not in keeping with my role to be left quite alone not knowing your whereabouts as head of the household.'

'Let me tell you, Beast, that as head, I have no call to let you know where or when I go away.'

John Jocelyn began to raise his voice and the dog barked. The monkey stared, the gryphon glared.

'Oh, but you do,' countered Miss Beast, acknowledging with a nod of her head her beastly army, 'because not to know is to undermine my teaching of the children. Your trust is their trust. I know that your visit was not as visits should be. These days have been dark for us all.'

As she spoke, John Jocelyn's round face was raised up from its careful collar on a thin neck. As it thrust itself towards her, to peck and bite, she clapped her hands to say, 'Go'.

The six creatures jumped down, scampered, prowled towards the master of the house and circled him. As they gathered round, Miss Beast realised that they could not attack. They each held defensive shields and no weaponry. She held neither, but she moved forward to synchronize the six, the winged, the clawed, the hoofed, with her pale, delicate, reader's hands. There would be a skirmish by the log pile, a fight in the hall, a duel beneath the brass light around which they circled. They'd circle, spinning with ease as the mistress of them all gave them their way. His dark thoughts of the beast came up to her on two legs, in suit, jacket and neck-tie, in the manner of a Judge and a scorner of peace.

'How dare you question my lineage and authority, Beast. This you will regret!' shouted John Jocelyn, and his head spun round in the collar to spit at each animal in turn.

She watched him spin uselessly until his venom spat no more, then she, too, turned with her creatures up the stairs to her rooms, alighting, jumping and swinging on to their appointed newel one by one as she passed.

Her room door closed firmly and Beatrice was looking down from her high bed. Alice was kneeling by the fire in the light of another day.

'Oh, Miss Beast, how bright your rooms are on this clear morning. It's December 1$^{st}$, and I've got the day off.'

# Sylvia's Garden

Delia did not really like her name and neither did her friend, Sylvia, like hers. It must have been the way in which their name was called by mother or teacher when they were at a distance, emphasising the two ending syllables 'ia' as if they were especially there to speak of their naughtiness or slowness or their being in the wrong place.

Sylvia was called to piano practice, always from a distance at the bottom of the garden. Delia was shouted at to come up from her favourite running game in the Flats' playground. But one interest brought them together, the school garden.

Gardens deny you before accepting you. It's as clear to the gaze of a seven year old as to one of seventy. At seven years, Delia was given her little patch of school garden. She was young in her year but quite tall, so Miss Carter allowed her to use the gardener's rake always kept out at the top of the slight incline near the shed.

'Sylvia can help you a bit at first because she's the oldest in the class,' she said and left Delia to look at the brown earth.

The two long-legged girls stood together, not so much looking as smelling, as every gardener does. What came to their nostrils could not be put into words then, but that first sniff of their garden would define each school term, each opening of a new school year, when Sylvia had her birthday, and its closing, when Delia had hers. It would open other events too, both real and imagined, of their lives together and apart, as best friends in that garden.

How did this plot quite close to central London come to know of gardens and gardening? Quite easily, replied the artisans of an earlier London growing rapidly along the River Lea with its market gardens, soft water for leather, cordwainers and cobblers. Soil spoke to them along the riverside of all the exotic fruit and flowers that would be grown. A gardener would appear, able to advise the newly moneyed who moved to Hackney, Highgate and Hampstead. This patch had a history of which Delia knew nothing, except that, when digging in the shade, there was a chill and a good reason to rise and scuttle her feet away.

'Sylvia, does anything grow under that tree?' asked Delia.

'No,' said Sylvia, 'it's too old.' Her seven year old logic stood firm.

Gardens deny you an open-book world. They hide so much even from the well-respected, trained and experienced gardener. Delia did not know that, but now she had a garden when she didn't have one at home. She went up the slope to look and turned to face the school building and its playground. It was September and a bright day, but the garden was in shadow under its beech tree. She looked around her at all the other little patches of garden, each miniature allotments with self-seeded plants from every dying summer. There were michaelmas daisies and golden rod towering over most of the plots. They are a deliberately untidy looking plant for the untidiest time of the year. Neglect over the summer holidays had its compensations though, because bright, copper red lanterns waved in the light wind of this enclosed space. Chinese lanterns, she found out their name later, splashed colour every gardener envies to spite the duns and dull yellows of an encroaching Autumn.

Delia didn't have much notion of a lantern. But she did see that these hung instead of spiking upwards. They lighted the path by her feet instead of striving for the sun. Sylvia's fair curly hair could be seen clearly as she bent down over at her plot. Delia squatted at hers, not knowing that her dark, straight hair blended well with the school garden's first turn of fresh brown earth for the new term. This was no green Highgate, Hampstead, Richmond and Kew. How on earth was this small school plot squeezed into this tightly built up area of London? The little local Primary School, close to the Church and the park, must have been built on the earlier century's town gardens to explain that vast beech tree. The Victorian builders kept the soil free for the children and bombs hadn't scarred it as had happened close by. When Delia and Sylvia dug and watered, nearly fifty years of a warring century had gone by under that beech.

Delia was too young to have read of secret gardens. There was no manual but what teacher said and what the little girl saw and did. There was a small water tap at the gate and glass jars with string to hold them straight were used for watering. The little hands picking up the weeds remembered the coolness of that treasured space. Then, quite suddenly, one Autumn, there was more. Delia was asked a question by her friend.

It was Sylvia's eleventh birthday. The party was to be at her house, a house with a garden.

'You can come, can't you, Delia?' a now much taller Sylvia said to her. 'Your mum and dad know I don't live too far away.'

Of course she didn't. In London speak it was 'up the road and round the corner', a ground floor flat in a large house which made Delia's own home seem like a pocket handkerchief.

Delia walked up the road that day in September with her two younger sisters, chattering about the home they had never seen and the prospect of a Saturday afternoon party. It did seem a strange time for celebration, though term starting had been exciting enough, especially in this last year before a change of school. Steps went up to a giant porch and a dark green front door. Used to stairs in their block of flats, Delia ran quickly enough up, pausing to catch her breath at the top. These were open steps, more of an indicator of freedom than the enclosed concrete stairway she knew from home.

Sylvia's father opened the door. He was a friendly man and Sylvia had said her much older brother was going to be a policeman like him. Delia guided her sisters into a large, long sitting room which looked onto a garden as green as September would allow when yellow tinges were arriving fast.

The three of them joined the others. Party games began and food was handed round, not at table but with all of them seated on rugs on the floor. Delia felt as if she was in a palace. Later on, playing under the grand piano with her sisters, she imagined its legs as columns to hide behind, even when the length of the room was so inviting.

Inviting, but intimidating, the garden was theirs for the rest of the afternoon and every one of the children was turned out onto the lawn close to the house with its rabbit hutch, small swing and bicycle for the eleven year old daughter, Sylvia.

Delia went with one of her sisters to explore the garden. Enclosed as it was, it was a bit too strange to explore alone. Anyway, she had sisters where Sylvia did not and sisters go with you, almost everywhere. She made sure her younger sister was happy on the swing.

The garden path led off to a large vegetable patch on the left and raspberry canes looked forbiddenly neat to the right. Delia felt the space instantly. It curved round her as if she was in a bowl as she bent down to lift up some of the heavy marrows to see what was underneath. She'd never seen them growing before, nor yet eaten one. Her mother had to shop at a distance and carry everything up four flights of stairs. A heavy marrow would not have been on her shopping list for a family of five. Peas to shell and carrots to scrape were staple and potatoes quite good enough for everyone. Delia saw the Greengrocer's shop differently with her aspiring gardener's eye. She had only thought of vegetables on sloping shelves or in boxes with dampened lettering in blue ink, but here there was roundness, unevenness and the smell of earth with all the variety it could produce. She was surprised by a clean cauliflower so near to the dirt and stepped over the marrows to see it. It must probably be for Sunday lunch tomorrow, her practical streak told her and then she saw the half dozen cabbages.

'They must be for weekdays,' she thought.

Wrapped up in her thoughts, she jumped when her sister's arm pulled her to her feet.

'Are you coming with me all the way down?' she said.

'Oh, yes,' said Delia firmly.

After the vegetable patch, the garden was not a garden any longer but the wilderness which children find in books they read in bed. This sunny, flower-filled space was quite safe, thought Delia, 'because I can see the sky above and Margaret's sandals just ahead.' Margaret, her sister, was hidden by the towering late summer flowers, but Delia was looking down at her feet so as to determine the path.

Above them both waved Delia's favourites of the fading year, but so much taller than at school. Michaelmas daisies, golden rod spiked almost everywhere and those copper red Chinese lanterns brightened up the unclear path. They hung to show another patch to explore, as if the school garden was enlarged to almost frightening proportions. But children like the thrill of fear together and Delia stepped on until her hands were pushing at plants she knew nothing of and avoiding what seemed helicopter high thistles visited by every late bee in the place. They buzzed like their counterparts in the sky, bringing a vast cloudy world in reach. Thistle dust played in the sunlight, dandelion seeds travelled on an unseen wind just as clouds cross our sight. Looking up at the majesty of newness around her, Delia knew she wanted to understand Sylvia's garden. To explore was to understand.

Her sister seemed content to tag along, so Delia slowly disentangled herself from convolvulus with its pink trumpets and then a clump of faded overextended mallow to set out towards a shed on the right. It had a tree overhanging it, but was warmed by the afternoon sun.

'Wonder what's in here, Delia?' said her sister Margaret, touching the first man-made object of their jungle journey like an explorer having arrived.

''Spect it's rakes and things,' replied Delia, as she spotted a path alongside. 'There's more, look.'

Shadowed by tree and shed, a short mossy path definitely lead on. The garden swung round completely to the left at the end of the shed and opened out into an area where trees were planted. A spider web was in their way so Delia ducked, Margaret following her. It was a badly neglected small orchard in the middle of London; a warm, balmy, fruitful place with a scent of excitement.

'Let's take some back up the path,' said Margaret.

She meant the reddened apples which she saw on each of the short ragged trees. The girls hadn't seen apples growing ever before, but they did know apples fell to the ground, therefore they grow on trees, like crab apples in the park. Size and shape were of no consequence to them. They each had on a dress for the party, so it was easy to carry a few with the skirt held as a dip at the front. Some would be for Sylvia's birthday they reasoned and they might get to take some home themselves if they were given a bag.

The two girls wandered slowly back, hands holding their cradled cargo, unable to part the overgrown flowers for each other as frond after frond whipped across their faces and bodies. Margaret came up close behind Delia so as to be part of her bulk in weaving their way. Delia was burdened by the apples, but not by her thoughts. The two girls were walking into the sun as they returned and Delia's gaze was surrounded by a haze of mist, flower dust, midges, spider webs and the occasional butterfly. There was such movement as she moved. The school garden had been static, open and dependable; this one moved with you and she knew she'd never be able to shake it off, neither its dust nor its drenching sun.

They dropped apples onto the lawn when they returned, where they looked a small amount for the trek they had taken. Sylvia's father grunted that he hadn't seen them so red before and that apples shouldn't be picked before they were ripe, then cheerily got on with the swing pushing. This one day had to be dealt with and he'd got time off 'specially.

A special day had drawn to a close and there would be a few others to come even though the two girls were to go on to different schools where they would make new friends. Sylvia and Delia were each studious, as school had taught them to be. University was an option left to one side for it was just at that later point a truth of the time stood between them. It parted them more surely than the axe which split the apple trees that year so that flats could be built at the back of the garden.

'It's said Sylvia's in the family way,' said Delia to her mother. 'I found it out from Dan's best friend who comes to Youth Club.'

'So that's the end of that,' said her mother, concentrating on a bit of window cleaning round the flat. She was becoming quite anxious about Delia's marriage reception to be held in one small room. 'He is going to marry her, isn't he?'

Delia nodded and started to help her mother out. The way to clean the exterior of the window was to sit on the windowsill outside, with legs dangling inside and casement frame firmly down above the knees. Mother stayed in the room. The top flat window looked over the wartime allocated allotment space, grassed over for many years. Delia had her back to the communal garden, sitting well forward to the window, leaning slightly and carefully as she rubbed and sparkled up the panes.

Of course, she was looking at herself. Thinking of Sylvia's garden didn't matter.

'It must have happened in the garden,' she mouthed to mother, not wanting to speak loudly.

'Yes, probably,' her mother replied, almost inaudibly from inside.

When the day of the wedding came, Margaret, maid of honour, nudged her sister the bride, as they stood for photographs before the car took them off.

'Sylvia's across the road,' she whispered. 'She didn't come inside. She must have felt she couldn't.'

Sylvia's garden was along the same road as the Church. She and Dan had been married in a Registry Office a month before. The parents' large flat had a room given up as a bedsit for the pair while they considered their future. Dad was said to be very angry.

'Yes, she's got Dan with her,' replied Delia as she looked down at her bouquet. They were her flowers for the day. Sylvia should have them to mark her married life with Dan, but Margaret would catch them in the traditional way. Their almost golden whiteness glowed against the white brocade of her dress. Even if she had wished for sunlight with its delicate haze of midge and moth to remind her of those garden flowers, she would not have had time to look as she ducked her head into the wedding car. Instead, she waved from the car at all the gathered friends. Neither she nor Sylvia would return to any garden together. That same garden freedom which had opened a window on the world for Delia, had shut her friend Sylvia away behind a wall of shame.

# Titfer

A full train moved on through the outskirts of Manchester. Instead of an overflowing set of carriages where passengers slump on backpacks as if they are sympathetic rising humps on an unyielding floor, each carriage held an obedient array of travellers, taking every seat facing forward or backward, seeming content with their lot if not with the price of their ticket. Evelyn could see right down two, almost three, carriages of the layout and was glad that her son and daughter, changing trains soon for Uni after the Mothers' Day celebration in York, had each got a seat somewhere.

Somehow, Evelyn sat uneasily. It wasn't the number of people, although that was a bit surprising for the time of day, a sunny early afternoon in March, nor the gentleman asleep beside her, but the layout. She had been looking round carefully for most of the first half hour of the journey. In her carriage, a large proportion of travellers were separated from those who would have chatted all the way with them. It's not as if it's a coffee shop, she had thought. Finding a seat and the train on its way is all you need to think about. More thoughts travelled on in the oddly quiet carriage, where only the noise of the train was uppermost.

A bubble burst of conversation and laughter came from the far end of the next carriage. She saw some legs in jeans jut out from a seat into the aisle once or twice and a set of shoulders hunch quite often to speak across it. There was more action in the distance than close by.

'Awesome.'

The two young men were standing on Leeds Station platform.

'Yes, it was. There's nothing like a few,' replied Nathan, looking around.

'More than a few, eh, Nathan?' Josh said, taking his hands out of his pockets to point. 'See him?'

'See who?' said his friend.

'That guy, down there with the daft hat.' Josh replaced his hands in his pockets to deliberately look away.

'So what?' said Nathan and looked up at the time. A large clock was set up on a grey brick pillar.

'I'd like to get him if he's on our train,' said Josh.

'What the hell do you mean, get him?' Nathan was quite used to Josh in this mood. 'He's with family looks like.'

'Yeh, well.' Josh turned his back to the small family group chatting a few metres away. 'We'll see what happens on the train.'

'Oh, yeh,' Nathan pouted at Josh, 'what's a hat to you then? Prob'ly a Jew-boy - better not touch 'im!'

'No, he's not. He's just a posh bastard,' said Josh.

'Ha, and you from Didsbury?' laughed Nathan and pushed his friend with a shove in the chest.

'What about you then?' said Josh as he pushed him back, slightly overbalancing on the platform in doing so.

'What the..!' Nathan snapped as he swung Josh round to pull him out of the sight line of the hat.

'Let me go, you twat,' swore Josh and then, 'Sorry lady,' as he almost trod on a travelling bag on the platform. 'Come on.'

'I can't see us duffing him up in a crowd like this,' said Nathan, craning up to see how far the line of passengers on the platform extended. 'Let's get nearer if we can.'

James Talbot looked round from a conversation with his sister and saw two young men a little older than him making their way from group to group on the platform. They were using the waiting families as a cover and they looked cheerfully close to drunk. Josh was the shorter. His light blue jeans were topped with a wide red and white check shirt and loose grey jacket cropped at the waist. Nathan displayed a similarly tipsy body language to Josh, but, as the taller, he stooped a little towards his friend.

'Stop it, you silly bugger,' he murmured.

Then Josh could raise his voice as he and everyone else heard the train coming in on their platform. 'He's for it, and you're with me, or else.'

'Or else bloody what?' Nathan shouted to him as he zipped up his jacket and came forward to board the train.

Josh looked behind him to spot the hat further down the platform and the door of entry taken by the young man.

These two had caught Evelyn's attention briefly. Their jerky movements, even at a distance, were meant to threaten as well as being the result of a merry swig or two before the journey. Feeling edgy and stupidly over-protective at the same time, Evelyn got up from her seat and went down the aisle to cross the carriage join and check on her son and daughter. They weren't sitting together, but she spotted their dark heads of hair in seats not very close to the two young men. She eyed those two briefly. One looked up at her before saying something to his friend, who moved his feet out of the aisle. As she turned back, she'd forgotten to look, she thought, but of course her son's hat would be on the table in front of him.

'She's on the prowl,' said Josh.

'Who is?' Nathan had to bend across the aisle.

'The mother of the geek in the hat. She's on our tail,' Josh smiled broadly.

'Now Josh, we ain't going for mothers or sisters.' Nathan spoke in a low voice.

'No, I'm going to get it as soon as they start getting off. I'll chuck it to you and you run.'

'Hmm,' Nathan replied to Josh's confident smile. 'Depends on which station don't it?'

'Just watch.' Josh sat back to do just that.

Outside the window of the two carriages, the south Pennines shaped into view. The sun shone onto raised rocks and smoothed hills as if it was an old friend who had promised to visit every day until the mountain was no more. Evelyn looked out at the shading of green and grey and blue, each the colours of the minutiae of rocks and basking vegetation that covered the slopes and faces. There was one colour to define, another to hide and a sun's shaft of warmth to deftly mark the difference for every abiding insect. Most passengers idly looking out were used to the sometimes threatening closeness of stone in this hilly landscape. The train route was close to the hills and then, far from their receding patterns as the winding river dictated. It was most often underneath them, which brought closer by far all the weight of primeval darkness revealed by strip light in the railway tunnel.

Evelyn studied the numerous passengers reflected in the black glass. Each looked at themselves first, then became aware of the others, the full train and even its speed, which was more difficult to gauge in the mirroring dark. When the light sprang back, almost everyone shifted or moved something close by on the table in front of them. Possibly her son touched his hat, her daughter looked to the leather backpack which was a present when she began at University.

Josh and Nathan had no bags with them. They'd been on a Saturday trip to friends, overnight on the couch and then back home when they could finally stand up. Nathan had glanced at the moving dark and leaned across to Josh.

'Not far now.'

'Just watch me,' said Josh, the dark making him whisper.

Not long after the train left the tunnel there was more movement. Legs were stretched. There were a few coughs and bags and coats were retrieved for the next stop.

Evelyn was pleased to have the first leg of the journey over, and a new view.

Josh and Nathan took their chance. As at the joust they set off down the aisle of the compartment. Josh nudged James sharply on the shoulder with a 'Sorry, mate!' and Nathan took the hat, shoved it on his head and pranced off to the train door which had opened onto Stalybridge Station.

He jumped down and looked around for Josh, preparing to leg it over the barrier, but Josh had encountered a problem, Evelyn.

Evelyn had come through from her carriage just in time to see exactly what Nathan and Josh were doing. She saw the lively thrust of a young man's shoulder, the wide hand coming down in a side swipe towards the table and all that through a muddle of clatter and movement as the train halted and people moved to leave.

'You two get your connection over the bridge,' she said to James as he turned to look for his sister. 'I'll get your hat back.'

'Mum, you can't do that,' James said, straddling the gap. 'It doesn't matter. I could see they were after it. It's only an old one.'

'I'm going after them,' said his mother.' They can't get away with stealing, just like that.'

'I'll 'phone Transport Police for you. 'Phone us,' called James and he guided his sister along the platform towards the local connections. They both looked back at their mother who had turned away quickly to find Josh in a tightly packed queue at the exit barrier.

'Excuse me,' she said as she found him at the door of the Station looking round for his friend. Josh was moving from one foot to another as he saw his cover of persons moving off up the station road into the small Pennine town. Just a couple of girls were left waiting for a taxi or a pick up. He needed to look as if he knew where he was going or knew what he was waiting for, so he turned with an air of determination to see who was stopping him.

'You took my son's hat and I want it back,' Evelyn said to the slight, clean shaven, casually dressed young man she had in front of her.

'What d'you mean, lady?' came the reply.

'I mean, you and your friend snatched my son's hat from his table where he was sitting on the train, and your friend's run off with it. I want it back.' Evelyn kept her eyes on Josh as he replied to her.

'Strikes me he ought to have had it on, then it wouldn't have got lost.'

'I don't need your cheek. Your friend took it and you know where he is. All I want is the hat back or I'll call the Transport Police,' said Evelyn sternly and stood even closer to Josh to make her point.

'I don't know where my friend or the hat is,' said Josh uncomfortably now. Apart from the Ticket Collector who had one eye on their conversation, there were just the two of them standing in the cheerless concourse in the north lee of the station.

'So, we'll wait until he comes back for you and brings the hat.' Evelyn only moved a fraction as she spoke.

'Yes. No, lady, he hasn't got the hat you're talking about. I don't know anything about it.' Josh stepped backwards as he spoke.

Evelyn immediately moved closer. All her instincts for self-preservation had Josh's own anxieties added to them. She was attaching a defiant bond. Like anyone in espionage, she knew he couldn't have worked alone, so she worked on his aloneness.

'Of course he's got the hat and he's left you here to pay for it,' snapped Evelyn. 'What kind of a friend is that? Can't you get on your 'phone and tell him I want him back here with the hat and I won't make any more fuss.'

Josh looked blank at her suggestion. He'd never used his 'phone for something like this. His reply was made for him. A text message buzzed on a mobile 'phone in the back pocket of his jeans.

'There you are,' said Evelyn, 'Now I'll see you answer it.'

Josh let the buzzing stop then lifted the 'phone from behind him to clumsily hold it in his hand. As he read it a faint smile crossed his face.

'No tricks now. You're staying here until your friend comes and I'm making sure of that.' Evelyn stood a little back from Josh as he tapped back what looked like a brief message. She hoped it was, 'Get back here,' but it was more likely to be, 'Get me out of here.' One thing was certain. She was aiming to stand her ground in front of Josh until the Transport Police arrived. Josh had just put his 'phone back when the Ticket Collector came through the Station's double doors.

'You Mrs.Talbot? They say they'll be half an hour.' He looked at Josh as he spoke. 'We'll see what happens then.'

Josh looked carefully at Evelyn as she briefly watched the man return. He made a move towards the road, but Evelyn got between him and the pavement edge, daring him to push her or run off. He stopped, patted his back pocket and stood very tautly before stepping back.

Evelyn decided to harangue.

'You two shouldn't have planned this in the first place. Why can't anyone have the safe journey they pay for without two like you getting up to silly pranks? A railway carriage isn't a playground and neither is it a place to steal anything that takes your fancy. You can't just walk off with other people's belongings and think they'll take it all in good part. Taking is stealing and that's a serious offence. What would your mother say if she saw you here now and me having to tell you what you already know?'

Evelyn made it a fair rant and locked her gaze on Josh as she spoke. He looked uncomfortable, alone, afraid. Evelyn saw, to her relief, that he decided not to be antagonistic but cunning. She didn't mind that at all. It was just what she was feeling herself, a manipulator of a situation which could go either way. Josh wasn't shouting. He seemed unable to settle his mind as he stood in front of Evelyn, but stand in front of her he did. He had the view onto the dismal open road, she the tunnel-like doorway of the small station entrance. Evelyn had never dealt with a stranger so personally and to restrict his freedom seemed most personal indeed. Josh shifted uneasily in front of her for the next ten minutes, stepping backwards occasionally as if he needed a bit of breathing space. Evelyn seemed to have him on a leash, so far to shift, circle, but no further. She'd never seen anyone so undecided about the passing minutes. He was waiting, but there was no watching He didn't look over her shoulder or round to the open station door. He was like a puppet expecting a firm shift to right or left, but it didn't or wouldn't come. There was no answer to that for the moment. He had all the affected nonchalance of someone waiting for a taxi outside a pub or a night club, but there were several ingredients missing from this mix. There were no friends, no mates, no chattering girls, no city sounds. He was a sinewy character but he faced her and showed nothing but worry. 'Phone reception in the hilly area was poor, they both knew, so it was a waiting game.

Josh spoke to her. 'I don't know why I did it. If I did it,' He sounded plaintive and brash together.

'Let's go onto the platform,' Evelyn suggested and followed Josh closely as they walked. It opened up to a long stretch of grey tarmac with a view of the hills opposite. She didn't look away from him for long. Just as she had hoped, his 'phone buzzed again. He got it out, looked at the text, looked at Evelyn and looked at the Station clock. Evelyn caught all this and guessed the escape route she'd given him by the deal in texts. Perhaps she knew it was for the best. A silent Josh stood beside her putting his hands in and out of his pockets. She wondered what he saw of her, not what he thought of her. They were both stereotypes, caricatures. How many close to drunk young men would be shifting slightly on station platforms all over England and how many mothers with sons would be making a plea for sanity, for the boy in the man to come back from playtime to wash his hands before tea?

She wished that the Police would come soon. She'd explain she'd got only one of the culprits and that the other had stolen the hat. Like her, Josh was busy with his own thoughts, possibly hoping that she would be busy with hers. The wind came sharply across from the nearby hills, not cold, but as a warning of the movement of weather, a shift in circumstance. It had been nearly thirty minutes now, a stressful half hour keeping a young man in one place with just a lot of chat, sharp looks and staring, all for a prank, stealing the hat, or a principle. Josh's eyes were blue.

Evelyn saw Josh moving down the Station platform. It was just a movement or two to idly look at the advertisements, then he strolled a bit farther off. She let him go, although she couldn't know of the open gate at the side of the platform of which his text had informed him. Josh disappeared through it and a second later Evelyn looked up to see the empty platform ahead of her and the sky between the hills ahead of that. Her blue-eyed boy had gone.

'Good,' she breathed and turned to walk back to the Ticket Office.

'He just got away,' she told the Collector, who had that second put the 'phone down.

'Police are on the next train, they say. They'll tell you about knives and such. You'll see. They'll say you shouldn't have done all that on your own. It was a long old time giving him tit-for-tat like, wasn't it?' He indicated a bench as he spoke to her.

'It certainly was.' she replied.

# Thirty Three Good Mornings: an Office Kim's Game

If you relish a morning by morning challenge, like a run in the park, seamlessly getting the children to school or completing a poo-perfect dog walk, then try this. You are taking thirty three trips to an office door. Each time a friendly good morning is replaced with a wordless greeting. Be ready with your invisible tray for the Kim's game, collecting an object from the office desk 'good morning' by 'good morning'. You'll have to remember them all at the end, but not in the way you would think. This is a meaning and memory challenge for all those who brave the graceless greeting for mornings, greetings with only half an ounce for the day itself and adding a hundredweight to yours.

An office door stands open.

Hold your tray ready. We shall begin with a filing cabinet moment. The 'good morning' goes straight into the fully extended drawer, echoed in the space where the hand goes for the item always lodged just there. There is the locus of us all and the impossibility of a 'good morning' when its complete exhalation is confined to the inconveniently mysterious. Were the accompanying thoughts for each daily object going to be like that, not so much oblique as confusing in an awkward disarmingness, instead of conveying what is usual in a morning, its just and varied good for all who take the trouble to look? Was the greeting to be self-directed, just as the arm caught in the filing cabinet, poking down the back as a small child might engagingly look for an escaped chocolate button?

No, we know about chocolate buttons. It's so difficult to find, lost chocolate. The little bag bursts. There goes the camouflaged brown penny piece, blending in with fenders if you go back a generation or more, or bureaux, patterned carpets, typewriter keys. The belief that it will be found, an elusive chocolate button, remains. Some even believe they know how many are in the packet, having spilled a proportionate number and, counting back in a split second, have the number that the factory machine would have spat into every little bag. After the filling came the sealing. A mind can be sealed just like that with yes, another 'good morning' - not snapped shut, just sealed with thoughts and feelings counted in and there to be portioned out for the day. This is chocolate button greeting, parsimonious as a clean factory floor with nothing for the minutiae which invisibly inhabit it when factory feet are gone.

So, that's the filing cabinet and chocolate buttons dealt with. Is there to be anything else? A desk life might go with a book, the book you want others to believe you are reading. The book whose covers attract more than the screen saver glare, usually with a bold type face. The 'good morning' book then has a one word title, conundrum enough to comment upon if comment were required after the 'good morning' makes comment obsolete. The word's had it then? 'Good morning' take one.

Which one will it be, 'good' or 'morning'? Let's picture no one walking away with 'good'. Quite quickly it's a wish that the take-away sum had given you 'morning' because 'good' is an extremity of thought, not found easily in the pocket. 'Morning' only needs to last a day in its rumination as a new morning will come tomorrow if morning has any meaning at all.

The next 'good morning', too, equated the sum rather thankfully, which was a strange fourth, unexpectedly harmonious since the greeting was given with a pencil in hand, thoughtful as a conductor 's baton raised over the desk to a tuneless auditorium of overnight dust caught by the early sun's rays and not likely to be obedient to a wooden stick. Casting round for a tune makes for a light step onwards. How about 'Lillibullero'? It's such a simple tune until it speeds to a maddening race accompanied by fancy additions and whirls of sound coming from a plucked air. The invisible dust of the office challenges the tune and refuses to settle properly. A few sneezes and the harmony is lost and a low drumming inhabits until the next daylight.

There follows the paperclip circus. Rummaging for a paper clip in a small pot, smaller than it should be for the size of finger or fingernail is like searching for water on Mars. A robotic hand needs to extend to such a tiny, precious commodity, lifting the molecule, which is the paper clip, required to bond the important paper together like $H_2O$. So that's a neatly scientific 'good morning'. A chemist isn't required to see the amount of moisture-filled breath exhaling over the detail of a paperclip, but the hunt is universal. They don't stay stuck on a moist finger but fall back into the untidy molecular maze which they represent in their pot at every level.

It's clear no-one on earth has invented a sticky note for 'good morning', but poised on a finger more securely than the gravity-loving paperclip, it charms nevertheless. It cannot greet. It can only remind and admonish, correcting to 'make this morning good'. If you were able to make a morning it could only be good and First Year Philosophers might find its goodness useful to aid discussion. How else would this small, square, colourful object influence at all? It's so easy to apply its nonsense stickiness to an object and change it forever. Perhaps Eden should have had a few sticky notes and certainly one on the apple, well applied, flapping in the gentle breeze or, more likely, prized off by the warmth to fall feebly and unnoticed to the ground.

When the morning came for the punched hole, there was a jauntiness about it. Perhaps the two holes wouldn't match, so the hole-punch was up-ended on its metal base in adjustment, resembling a carriage lurching lopsidedly on a funicular railway in some far off resort. When off balance is really treated it is the pleasure of security it brings. Any mountain climber knows this, that lurching from secure foothold to planned footfall is mesmerising and individually unique. If the hole-punch can speak to us of insecurities, not in its solidity of form, but in what, as an object it insecurely does, wobbling its way to the straightened paper and just as likely to miss as the rest of mankind, then risk-taking hole-punch management courses ought to be applied for with an exceptional take up rate.

It is the staple of every morning, its 'good' or goodness and there is very little that is good about a staple. What else lets fly in unimaginable directions, fits two sheets together only to find a third unattached, and cannot be re-used in any shape or form? So it is with the stapler's 'good morning', set to with gusto, palm of hand on the staple arm, confidence in the morningfull of staples and a primed machine anxious to do the will of the day. Like all machines in existence, however eager to do one's bidding, the right degree of obligation is required. Often, for the stapler user, it is a requisite to rise slightly from the office chair to apply pressure or the stapler spins into a circus act, immediately falling flat, having received no training from the clown. It creases priceless paper and tampers with ego and a clown's down-at-mouth painted on mouth's width turns to the audience to placate. There is never a good morning to fall flat on your face and best of all not with an office stapler in your hand.

I've been wanting to talk to you about that pen, though. It's the one which makes writing easy, no mess, no blots, ball-pointed and smooth. That's why it's picked up for a thoughtful 'good morning' which a keyboard tap or two won't do. It adds more to the e-mail that a note has been made on the lips by the tap of a pen. 'I must remember this alert opening again'; this more prominent 'good' perhaps, or is touching the lips a nod to the stars, which, we are told, started off these mornings in the first, or was it last place? Lips to cold metal top so as to kiss a rosary bead or as a wedding ring is turned, meaning much in the littlest movement, the twist, the exalting touch. A 'good morning' for the heavens and all its stars and planets with a pen poised on the lips.

After that an ordinary pencil sharpener looks a petty piece of officeness more often hidden in a drawer or pot than scrutinised in this good manner this morning. Was it emphasising the circularity of the opening, defending the jet engine heat from such a small conical furnace, or the sharp side made like a safety razor blade of the Thirties? Probably it was an enlarging principle at work. A giant jet engine now heats the office, blasting it away to your next holiday in Teneriffe, where the wind blows softly and gently on to a stressed life of looking into sharpeners for the lost lead. Better still let it blow in to the draughty air of the back shed of an aircraft factory. That's really where you need the pencils and sharpeners, for those sitting at desks in years of planning at drawing boards. It is just the littlest of things which blows you away.

Now, with leaden dust settled and portion of graphite dropped in the office bin, a 'good morning' is as becoming as a smile when the photo frame is caressed. The digit raised to the outline of the frame, curved or straight or raised with fretwork atop. 'This frames the photo nicely' means, makes it a whole in a limiting landscape, mutes the photo out of its truth of taking be it wedding day or local bar and renders it a piece of fantasy. Why else should the best frames be silver or wood, taken from the elements as if to disguise our focused milliseconds here? Digit has now caressed frame and the action is over except that the observer now takes the framing in to a limitless day. What frames there are for our attention. The best are inlaid woods of all description, even ebony, gracing desk and table tops the world over, from pot boys to palaces. This is a constantly curvaceous 'good morning', taking the fancy on a ride to the Punjab, where, on the top of a lorry a frame encloses a god with its stunning caress.

Then the doodling on a notepad which hardly takes 'good morning' to the surrounding air. Only the jerk of the script brings it to you in joined up swirls of 'ohs'. They look very sweet pushing together just as cumulus clouds jostle to demand you enjoy the fresh cauliflower look of them all. The sky too, can market its wares. But let's centre up to the jotter pad marketing only a disjointed phrase like, 'let Meg know'.

'Meg, Margaret, Maggie and me, have been invited out to tea,' but only if the 'good morning' came off the pad to let us know. It'll stay there, blurred by too few thoughts of Meg and decidedly no thought of know.

If you can identify a mugshot at a glance as an old time Copper had to do, you might think that the same thing applied to a mug. Glance at the mug, know the mug, in the Copper's lingo, but no, wait, persevere with thought. The logos never mean what they say or say what they mean, just like this mug-held 'good morning'. Every picture, every logo and phrase spits out that you've been manipulated into holding this and you cannot make it your own however humorously hard you try. That is the mug, not the mugshot.

It's certainly taking advantage to wave a handwritten letter in greeting as it waves you away to deal with bills and flyers. Who wouldn't enjoy the purely handwritten, joyed in, pen flowing, something thoughtful to write? And thoughts need to be expressed if only through the 'good morning' process. Are you not close enough to spot whether card or sheet inside, so the cry goes up, 'Can good morning have a birthday?' Of course it can.

'It's thirty three today, hip, hip hip hooray'.

There's no sign of celebration for such an odd birthday, if so it was, from the handwritten letter, so perhaps inside is the greeting 'good morning' waved aloft to signal that it can be written as well as spoken. Now we have written, spoken gesture held aloft in cream laid self - adhesive pack of fifty sent from a well-meaning great aunt who has lost home address but has knowledge of job in an office and found a postcode. Improbable to the final magic 'e', it's really a filed away envelope finally unearthed and waved in derision to the few pence paid years ago for the stamp.

Animal, vegetable and mineral green, short and dangerous is a treasury tag scratching a neat wooden or leather desk lethally. Here it is now, attached to a thick document raised up to check that sending this would break the bank. What's treasured up there? The tray is almost half full now of desky treasures each fulfilling its theme tune attempting 'good morning' in mercifully delightful ways. Had the treasured tag been dug from a dusty tomb its joining stem would have powdered into earth leaving a query about two identical pieces of clasped-over soft steel. Are they pins to set at the ears; a twin stand for a minute dish of perfume, being uses far beyond the inch measure they contain? The archaeologist's guess is far less secure than the tag's, carbon dated to modern desk time.

Now the bulldog clip is a perfect tool for desk play. Sit it upright 'stay, stay', and two small rims of steel like bulging cheeks wobble with trusty obedience. Lay it down and an uncomfortable lack of symmetry from wrong angle or wrong place evokes sympathy. So do we have a sympathetic 'good morning' after taking the dog for a walk? The steely object awakes a certain pride in a job well done with full security between clenched teeth which will open wider, wider to bark, 'good morning' until shut in the filing kennel.

We'll find a tool for a job which not one of your ten fingers can do for long and need look no further than a thimble. This, encrusted with rubberised bristles beats and bats at paper until it flies off the pile in a whirlwind. Slow down and the old blue numbers of Edwardian indexing ghost each corner of the slow motion counting. Clerks did this before typewriter madams elegantly numbered pages and absolved the male from meticulous ledgers. The humble thimble's appearance in the box file culture reminds a too bright office of its four o'clock light forbears and of worn out thimbles counting sheaves to the day's end. That makes a sunset of the 'good morning' but with a great deal more light to shed than in current times, counting out the cost of the letters of 'good morning' as if there was a prize for the best comptometer of the week.

A measured 'good morning' with a ruler sounds like the purring of a cat as it adjusts front paws on 'good' and stretches up and back with front legs extended and caught in the carpet as if yawning of a 'morning'. If there was a 'good morning' rule, cats aside, then it might be never to measure the distance between the adjective and the noun because then the straight metal bar placed on the tray would have to be a spring. Maybe an old bed spring would do, with tension enough in grandpa's very old bed to take his weight for every good night and his last night, from which his final measured, good, morning would lead to box and earth and time, all measured quite differently. The cat would curl up to protest.

This next 'good morning' was easily erased from the mind, in fact, it was being vigorously rubbed out at the moment of speaking as if, at this halfway point in passing the office of all mornings, be they good or not, all previous visits were to be obliterated. So there go half the thoughts on the tray, winged away on an airbrush of rubberised particles joining all other items of office dust in a million years' long attempt to create a lunar landscape. The full extent of obliteration is never evident to us all. Not even after the largest of tsunami waves is there nothing at all. Sand hides county-sized dunes which shift overnight to reveal more than the weight of sand which left and any hole dug in earth's patient soil can never un-become a hole. It dents, as every action dents our lives for good or ill. Erase away a beautiful morning - it cannot work.

Completing the Moebius 'good morning' a rubber band will stretch out the day until the day can be elongated no longer. Unlike the stretching cat with its limiting limbs, this band will reach all the way to the most incriminating task of the day which then slides down it to land with uncompromising discernment back on the desk in-tray. Never take a rubber band seriously, however much harm you know it can do, for in springing back into life it will snake around and meet you reaching for that apple.

What hard task masters these are, the scissor-said 'good mornings', glinting on the golden air! If ever there was 'hand-held' this is it. See how they mimic the fingers' scissor movement, cutting sharply fine what soft flesh alone delivers to plucking a flower or lifting a child's buggy to the boot - a one scissor grip finally and faultlessly consigning young lives to the confines of a car. Neat and nice, the desk scissors cut the air, extending the hand to the shake of a steely 'good morning' now lost in Sheffield's smoother trams and noisy hillside starts.

When the pen pot is emptied of its pen, pencil and the scissors which sat like pince-nez rakishly peering onto the desk, CCTV pen pot swivels over the desk top, producing a grey jerky scene of desk ballet daily. Rewind and play forward to test the swivel area of the pot's range. Wrist comes into view. 'He was sprawled on desk with wrists keeping the swivel chair from colliding with the wall. I'd say a gun was being aimed at close range and wrist language points to this', writes tape assessment. What age would bring about a nightmare of Super Sister's spectacles watching your desk debris and lonely tapping paper clip? Only the bleakest of 'good mornings' brings this about. How is community destroyed but by reportings on the desk top, like washing on the line. Spy on pen-pot and create a new world order, or by your temerity of pottiness ensure a mild query brings us all a lap full of laughs.

That roving mouse will cheer all in its company as it runs you into unknown worlds and makes 'taking a mind for a walk' into a moonlanding exercise. But look at what the mouse pounces upon, neatly negotiating the small space of creep, retreat, forward and jump. Mouse playing cat isn't unknown at all. We've nearly cleared the desk of items for pouncing on. Few items remain for the tray which awaits them and their unspoken thoughts for the day. Our mouse nibbles on the car keys then drags them on an imaginary journey down mousehole, along wainscot and under floorboards like all its forbears.

How clinking keys quickly disappear. Keys which take you everywhere but into the enquiring mind where 'good morning' feints and fancies it has the key to all future 'good mornings'. It will unlock a drawer full of musing, instead of the vast globe of difference requiring every key in the universe to unlock its gates on any morning, never mind a good one. There they go, the silently clinking keys. They solidify on the tray in a collapsed, carved and unique mass. There is an occasional jerking of the core, as if Etna's solidity is not real. The jerking key is the one that no longer fits a lock, but remains on the ring to taunt and tease. It's slightly slippery and ill at ease, keeping out of the limelight in the key's core, ready to make its malign insignificance felt.

Then there's that more sinuous 'good morning'. It's with spectacles case just shut, hands on the liquid lined box to replace where best to remember. Hearty heat waves come across from its warm curves, along with the radiant vision of shades, which shall be boxless as they perch on the head, worn in Teneriffe, Torbay, Tenochtitlan, wherever fancy takes the shaded eye. In the case study of early morning heat, the greeting comes as if to warm the sand or, if that's a tallish order, given the god already risen, toward the lounger, striped, with awning and sides of hand through sand, hand in hand with sun-lounger adjacent.

A hapless memory stick is a non-starter as a 'good morning', as it has no pre-programmed memory of this 'good morning' greeting or of its own. Intended to hold, it very tenaciously fits its fine place and, plugged in for this morning, quite clearly relishes its lack of feeling for today, for it needs to be told that today has begun. Tortuous little enterprises these sticks, stylised to ostentation and busy doing nothing but marking every click of teetering lives. What 'good morning' then with this little fellow, unaware that it had begun? A blessed one indeed, for we cannot go where memory has not gone and to start from blank is a blankness to us all.

That box of staples to refill the stapler has appeared this morning gripped with an elegant frenzy. This is small box 'good morning' served with a hitch of the shoulders that such a small machine needs a service. 'Chug, chug, splutter', goes the engine when inevitably few staples rest on the silver plinth, our never being able to consider the next push and snap of nothing there. Hence the full box, the slightest odd pressure on the cardboard, the tiniest sweat that they are the right size and the 'good morning' might be given with all the components in place, and that'll be a first on behalf of all who own a full box.

Look, there seems to be a piece of card peeping out of the one word-titled book. 'Ouch' by S. Interest, it was, bold as brass, taking the shine off 'good morning' on an earlier morning. It's bookmarked for level of devotion and direction to the subject and the eloquent author. There is always a typing error on page 100 as is frequently observed, rather as if a century of words is quite enough without more to carry on. This piece of card flipped the 'good morning' over the desk top. A ladybird must have landed for another take-off and she'd been winged on her way before the wheels were down. What a thoughtful bookmark to provide the rest from labour, the place in the sun, the end of the runway?

Then, this one blots, is often engraved and is seen far less often than a hopping garden bird. Here it is 'good morning' with its dark, smooth lines on the desk ready for important and immediate action. Primed as it is, it describes a morning as nothing else does. It must be ready to erupt, as dawns do, ready to write, as a morning does immediately on our hearts, until ready to flow, to move rapidly over the paper of the day, effortlessly and fluently with special and unique intent. This is a humble instrument designed for the Maker's work indeed and evolution has given it that cachet of excellence which shines as bright as day. A Will is to be witnessed, a Charter signed and the magnanimity of the morning is universal no longer but historically penned and primed into the collective consciousness of the named.

This well-made paperweight should be boxed then opened for show, not deliberately raised as in this 'good morning' to catch the light and wave it to the eye. Glass or resin enclosed millefleurs glimmer momentarily like flowers on an alpine field or violets in early Spring. Would a flower so weighty be as dexterous as this? Perhaps it would be balanced on a bamboo stick in some far forest like a Clown with a plate, wobbling for the giant hoverfly settling for its saucer full of dew. The dewed morning makes its weight settle on to paper pile from which no larvae will hatch, no dew be squeezed and weighted paper will worry us no more.

Watch white correcting fluid correct no other way than to help us imaginatively leap through snowy passes of mistakes. With goggles on and skis ready, the attack on the sinuous whiteness commences. It is an ugly white and globularly undrying, whilst cleansing snow leaks into boots to say a friendly, 'hello'. The 'good morning' is not frosty, white or crisp, but finally found to be faulty all along, and there is not enough fluid in the little pot. From what acreage would come the whiteness to glow away the other mornings, whose objects fill the tray to end the tale?

The desk is almost clear and a calendar remains. Month by month it is for over two thousand years and opened at June for no obvious reason. Looking laconically at holidaying hours, perhaps, or re-writing the rhyme:

Thirty days hath September,
June and August, then November.
What if June had thirty-three
Branches on a Juniper tree?

Calendar, sundial, scratch clock, make your mark on the day. Point your shadow to the dawn of a brighter day and the goodest morning. To praise it endlessly consider this different figure at the office desk. A quill is laid aside and a cowl shaken off. In obedience, no 'good morning' is spoken for Mattins has yet to be sung.

Now for the tune of the story, your story, whether or not you pass this office by each day. How many drawers had the filing cabinet? Thirty two items more on the tray for you to remember a new something about them, to take you beyond the fainthearted object-waving greeting no-one should endure. Did that chocolate button break in half? Is the book paper or hardback? Can you tell whether it is an H or 2B pencil, and what colour the paper clip and sticky note? What about the two-holed hole punch, or was it four, and the size of the stapler, long armed or not? Was the ball point plastic or steel and likewise the sharpener along with the photo frame, plastic, silver or wood? Make a picture of the tray from this exercise. Was the notepad lined or plain and the mug as deliberate a colour as the stamp on the letter, do you recall? Did the tag have plastic ends and what size is the bulldog clip? How pliable is the thimble, the ruler brass or steel, how white the eraser, how long the rubber band and the scissors how sharp? Remember the pen pot which remembers you? Is it round or square for mouse to enquire 'whose am I?' Taking further stock and very pleased with ten to go the race is on to find the number of keys on the ring, the colour of the glasses-case, the memory stick's miniaturisation and the amount on that full box of staples. Nearly there. Now then, bookmark width in centimetres, smart inkpen maker's name and circumference of paperweight should slow you down to completion; then, is it fluid corrected with sponge or brush, calendar illustrated or not? Tie-breaker time. 'What is it written by the dove-feather quill on this morning's white page?'

Lightning Source UK Ltd.
Milton Keynes UK
UKOW03f0942050114

223988UK00010B/226/P

9 781845 496012